My fingers encircled my amulet, and my worry grew stronger. I *should* be able to stop time using the black stone at its center, go invisible, and do all sorts of things, but the last time I tried some experimentation, I had nearly destroyed myself. But if I didn't do something . . .

Barnabas put his hand around mine, both of us holding the shiny black stone that kept me looking alive, and I turned to him, blinking in surprise. "I'll take care of this," he said, compassion in his deep brown eyes.

My lips parted, and I nodded. I didn't have to do this alone.

Also by **KIM HARRISON:**

Once Dead, Twice Shy

Something Deadly This Way Comes

EARLY TO DEATH, EARLY TO RISE

A NOVEL

KIM HARRISON

HARPER
An Imprint of HarperCollins*Publishers*

Early to Death, Early to Rise

 For information address HarperCollins Children's Books, a division of HarperCollins Publishers, 10 East 53rd Street, New York, NY 10022.

www.epicreads.com

Library of Congress Cataloging-in-Publication Data

Harrison, Kim.

Early to death, early to rise / by Kim Harrison. — 1st ed.

p. cm.

Summary: When Madison Avery, seventeen, spunky, and technically dead, takes on the role of Dark Timekeeper, she struggles to figure out her place in the war between light and dark reapers.

ISBN 978-0-06-144169-1

[1. Dead—Fiction. 2. Death—Fiction. 3. Future life—Fiction. 4. Fate and fatalism—Fiction. 5. Supernatural—Fiction. 6. Fantasy.] I. Title.

PZ7.H2526On 2009 2009026331

[Fic]—dc22

Typography by David Caplan

11 12 13 14 15 CG/BV 10 9 8 7 6 5 4 3 2 1

❖

First paperback edition, 2011

For Andrew and Stuart

Prologue

Seventeen, dead, and in charge of heaven's dark angels—all itching to kill someone. Yup, that's me, Madison, the new dark timekeeper without a clue. It wasn't exactly how I envisioned my "higher education" going the night I blew off my junior prom and died at the bottom of a ravine. I'd survived my death by stealing my murderer's amulet.

Now it's my responsibility to send a dark reaper to end a person's earthly existence. The idea is to save their soul at the cost of their life. Fate, the seraphs would say. But I don't believe in fate; I believe in choice, which means I'm in charge of the very people I once fought against.

The seraphs are confused about the changes I'm trying to make to a system I don't believe in, but they're willing to give me a chance. At least, that's the theory. The reality is a bit more . . . complicated.

One

The car was hot from the sun, and I pulled my fingertips from it as I slunk past. Excitement layered itself over my skin like a second aura. Hunched and furtive, I followed Josh in his first-day-of-school jeans and tucked-in shirt as he wove through the parking lot toward his truck. Yes, it was the first day of school, and yes, we were ditching, but it wasn't like anyone ever *did* anything the first day. Besides, I thought the seraphs would forgive me; it was one of their marked souls I was going to try to save.

Josh turned to me as he stopped, crouched behind a red Mustang as he tossed his blond hair from his eyes and grinned. It was obvious this wasn't his first time skipping. It wasn't the only time I'd ditched school, either, but I'd never done it with a posse. I smiled back, but as Josh's gaze went behind me, his smile faded.

"She's going to get us caught," he muttered.

My yellow sneakers with the skull-and-crossbones shoelaces ground into the pavement as I turned to look. Barnabas was skulking properly between the cars, his dark eyes serious and his expression grim. Nakita, though, was casually strolling, her arms swinging and her perfection absolute. She was wearing a pair of my designer jeans and one of my short tops, looking better than I ever could, with her dark hair shining and her black toenails glinting in the glorious sun. She hadn't painted them that color, it was natural. Normally I'd hate Nakita for her looks alone, but the dark reaper didn't have a clue how pretty she was.

Halting in a crouch beside me, Barnabas frowned, the scent of feathers and sunflowers coming off him. The angel masquerading as a high school senior in his faded black jeans and even more faded band T-shirt was twice fallen: first when he was kicked out of heaven untold millennia ago, and now for having switched sides in the middle of heaven's war.

"Nakita hasn't the faintest idea how to do this," the reaper grumbled, brushing his frizzy brown curls out of his eyes and squinting. The two had been on opposite ends of heaven's war, and it didn't take much to set them off on each other now.

I cringed, waving for Nakita to crouch down, but she just kept walking. Nakita was my official guardian, assigned to me by the seraphs.

Technically, as the dark timekeeper, I was her boss. Although in all things earthly I was the smart one, she knew my job and what I was supposed to be doing. Trouble was, I didn't want to do it heaven's way. I had other ideas.

"Get down, you ninny!" Barnabas hissed, and the petite, beautiful, and deadly girl looked behind her, confused. Over her shoulder was the trendy purse I'd given her this morning to complete her look. It matched her red sandals and was absolutely empty, but she insisted on carrying it because she thought it helped her blend in.

"Why?" she said as she approached. "If someone should stop us, I'll simply smite them."

Smite? I thought, wincing. She hadn't been on earth very long. Barnabas fit in better, having been kicked out of heaven before the pyramids were built because he believed in choice, not fate, but Nakita once told me rumor had it he'd been ousted for falling in love with a human girl.

"Nakita," I said, pulling at her when she got close, and she obediently dropped to a crouch, her long hair swinging. "No one uses that word anymore."

"It's a perfectly fine word," she said, affronted.

"Maybe you could try smacking people instead?" Josh suggested.

Barnabas frowned. "Don't encourage her," he muttered. Nakita stood.

"We should go," she said, looking about. "If you can't get the mark to *choose* a better path before Ron sends a light reaper to keep him alive, I'm going to take his soul to save it."

With that, Nakita started walking for Josh's truck. "Take his soul" was a nice way of saying "kill him." The enormity of what I was trying to do fell on me, and my shoulders slumped.

I was the new dark timekeeper, but unlike the dark keepers who came before me, I didn't believe in fate. I believed in choice. The entire situation was a big cosmic joke—apart from the bit about me being dead. The old dark timekeeper thought that killing me, his foretold replacement, would give him immortality. No one had known who I was until it was too late to change anything, and I'd been stuck with the job until I could find my real body and break the bond with the amulet that kept me alive without it.

Josh rose, peering at the parking lot's entrance through the Mustang's windows. "Come on. Let's get to my truck before she takes the front seat. I'm not driving with her riding shotgun."

Knees bent and keeping in a crouch, we started after her. Barnabas was vastly better at this soul-saving stuff than I was, knowing how to use his amulet and having experience finding people marked for an early death in order to save them from reapers like Nakita. That he had switched sides to stay with me was as weird as my being chosen as the new dark timekeeper to begin with. Maybe it was guilt that had kept him with me, since he'd failed to keep me alive when I'd been targeted for death. Perhaps it was anger at his old boss, Ron, the light timekeeper, who'd lied to both of us in his quest for supremacy. Or it might possibly be that Barnabas thought I had answers for the questions that Ron's betrayal had raised. Whatever the reason, I was glad Barnabas was here. Neither of us agreed with heaven's philosophy of killing someone before they went bad, but if I'd been fated to become the new dark timekeeper, I could've done far worse than win Barnabas's loyalty. Nakita didn't trust him and thought he was a spy.

"Uh, guys?" Josh said, and I froze when I followed his gaze to the squad car parked before the school. Beside it was a woman in uniform, hands on her hips and looking our way.

"Crap!" I yelped, dropping. Josh was right beside me, and Barnabas had never risen above the level of the car. "Get down!" I almost hissed at Nakita, and yanked her toward the pavement. My pulse hammered. Okay, I know. I was dead, but try telling my mind that. It thought I was alive, and with the tactile illusion of a body, who was I to tell it different? It was embarrassing. If I was simply sitting, nothing—but the minute I got excited, the memory of my pulse started up. It was so unfair that I had to deal with all the physical crap of being scared when I was already dead, but at least I didn't sweat anymore.

My back was pressed against the car we were hiding behind. Beside me, Josh looked worried. "It's Officer Levy. Do you think she saw us?" I whispered. Just freaking great, I was already on the woman's radar. She had tailed me speeding to the hospital when Nakita had almost killed Josh two weeks ago. Yup, she'd smited him, but only halfway. I wouldn't call the two of them friends, but at least Nakita wasn't trying to kill Josh anymore.

Crouched before me, Nakita started to rise. "I'll smack her."

"No!" both Barnabas and I shouted, tugging her back down.

Josh was peeping through the windows. "She's gone."

Son of a dead puppy. How am I supposed to save some guy's life if I can't even sneak out of the high school's parking lot? I'd told the seraphs that if I could talk to him—the mark—he would make a better choice and he wouldn't have to die to save his soul. This was likely my best chance to prove that my ideas could work. I didn't want to lose my opportunity by getting to the party too late. And I wasn't going to blow it all to dust because I was sitting in detention—and then my room after my dad found out.

My fingers encircled my amulet, and my worry grew stronger. I *should* be able to stop time using the black stone at its center, go invisible, and do all sorts of things, but the last time I tried some experimentation, I had nearly destroyed myself. But if I didn't do something . . .

Barnabas put his hand around mine, both of us holding the shiny black stone that kept me looking alive, and I turned to him, blinking in surprise. "I'll take care of this," he said, compassion in his deep brown eyes.

My lips parted, and I nodded. I didn't have to do this alone.

He and Nakita were here to help until I could do things myself. Seeing my gratitude, he smiled, and his hand slipped from mine as he stood.

"You?" Nakita barked as she stood, too. "If anyone is doing any smiting, it will be me!"

Josh sighed. "There they go again."

Barnabas's expression became peeved, but his eyes went wide as he focused behind her. A dry clearing of a throat shocked through me, and I stood when I saw Officer Levy with her hands still on her hips and disappointment in her expression.

"Isn't it a little early for a field trip?" she asked. She looked too young to be a cop, but the no-nonsense slant to her eyes demanded a respect that went beyond her snappy haircut and slim stature.

"Officer Levy!" I said, feeling foolish as I brushed off my skirt. It was black, with skulls and crossbones on the hem. It matched my shoelaces. And with the black tights, the outfit was out there, but all me. "Wow, it's good to see you again. I didn't know you were assigned here," I said.

My voice died, and no one said anything while she looked at each of us in turn.

"Ah, we were getting something out of Josh's truck," I lied, looking at it two aisles away—two aisles and six hours away. *Crap.*

Her eyebrows were high, and she took her hands from her waist. "Josh, Madison . . . and you two are . . . ?" she asked.

"Barney," Barnabas said, not looking up as his eyes silvered. He'd given her the name I used when I was mad at him, which told me he was ticked at himself.

"And you, young lady?"

"Nakita," the dark reaper said boldly as she fingered her amulet as if preparing to use it.

"She's my sister," Barnabas said, pulling her close in what Officer Levy would think was a sideways hug but what I knew was an admonishment for her to behave herself. Trouble was, they both thought they were top dog, and it only made things worse when she shoved him off her. "We're transfer students from Denmark," he added, and I looked at him in surprise.

I thought it was Norway. . . . "They're staying with me," I added.

Officer Levy seemed to relax, apparently satisfied with our downcast expressions. "You're going to be on probation if you pull this again," she said, dropping back and gesturing toward the school. "Inside. All of you. I'm not going to bust your chops the first day of school. Let's go," she said as she ushered us ahead of her, and as one, we pushed into motion.

"Sorry," Josh muttered as I came even with him, but whether he was talking to me or Officer Levy, I didn't know. Disappointment slipped into me, tinged with desperation. The hair on the back of my neck prickled as I heard Officer Levy behind me. *We're not going to go quietly, are we?* I thought, but the wink and sly smile I caught from Barnabas when I looked at him brought me straight with anticipation.

"Keep walking," he mouthed, then tugged Nakita's arm to bring her even with Josh and myself. I couldn't help but smile at her muffled complaint as Barnabas put his head next to hers and convinced her not to smite the woman.

"I saw what you were going to do," he said, his hand upon his amulet as it started to glow a faint green. It used to be ruby red, but since he'd abandoned his light-reaper status and gone grim, it had shifted up in the spectrum—much to Barnabas's embarrassment. "Smiting her has the finesse of a rhino, Nakita," he added. "You need to learn the art of minimization. Just watch."

Then, softer, to me, Barnabas whispered, "Madison, start to drop back until Officer Levy walks right past you. Josh, I'm sorry; I can't cover you. The woman has to take someone in. The best I can do is make it so you don't get in trouble."

Josh sighed, glancing at me as he took my hand. "I'll see you later," he said softly, his expression both unhappy and resigned. "I knew it was too good to be true."

My fingers slipped from his, and I winced. "Get my assignments for me?"

"Yeah. I'll stop at your house after school. Got my number?"

I touched my pocket, feeling for my cell phone. "Always," I said, and Nakita made a huff of sound, not understanding at all. Most everything was logic for her. That was the difference between her and Barnabas. For all his sourness, he was ruled by his heart.

I felt like dirt for ditching Josh, but what else could I do? Slowly I started easing my pace, both Nakita and Barnabas dropping back with me until Josh continued on ahead of us, his head down and his hands in his pockets. I held my breath as I shifted to the side and let Officer Levy walk right on past. Barnabas touched my elbow, and I stopped. His other hand was around his amulet, and his eyes were silver as he touched on the divine, changing Officer Levy's memories to not include us. It was a minor task, but one I think they were both reluctant to teach me because of what I might do with it. Sure, I was their boss, but I'd gotten the job without the lifelong apprenticeship and discipline that usually went before it.

I stood between cars and watched, unbelieving as Officer Levy seemed to forget all about us, escorting Josh back to the school as if he were the only one she'd seen. Reaper magic—you gotta love it.

"The woman will remember," Nakita said with a huff, hip cocked and watching, too. "You used so little of the divine that the false memory won't stick."

"It will stick long enough for us to leave, and that's all we need." Josh clearly forgotten, Barnabas took my elbow and directed me to the field at the edge of the parking lot, but my eyes were on the school behind us and the open windows. "And when she comes back to look and she finds nothing, then there will be doubt in her. A week from now, she won't remember it because it will be easier for her to forget."

A week, I thought, hoping he wasn't making a mistake. I had thought it would be more certain than that. Nakita, too, seemed unconvinced.

Shoulder-to-shoulder, we turned and left the cars behind us to walk out onto a long-fallow field thick with bees and tiny flowers. I couldn't help but feel odd as I walked between the two angels, one light, one dark, as if I were somehow connected with all the past that had happened before me and the future yet to be. If I hadn't known the school was behind us or smelled the pavement and hot metal, I could have been walking in Eden.

Nakita looked to the sky and shook her hair back. A smile so beautiful that it hurt came over her. As she stretched her arms to the heavens, her wings—her glorious, black-feathered, impossibly big wings—melted into existence, glistening in the sun. Dark reaper, dark wings.

Worried, I looked behind us to the school. When I turned back, Barnabas had found his wings as well. His were white, and I wondered if they would eventually change color like his amulet had.

I had less than twenty-four hours to try to help some nameless soul who was about to find himself at the center of a fight for his very life. *And we,* I thought as Barnabas wrapped an arm around my waist and I stepped backward upon his feet so he could carry me into the air, *are the only ones who can save him.* We were bringing both his salvation and his death . . . because if I couldn't convince him to make a different choice, Nakita was going to kill him.

Two

Fort Banks Mall was a wave of air-conditioned coolness. I could actually feel the heat of the sun leave me as I waited by the information stand for Barnabas and Nakita, who were currently having a hushed argument just inside the double glass doors. Grace, my onetime guardian angel now turned messenger, was humming somewhere above me. The softball-size glowing ball of light had joined us almost as soon as we'd gotten airborne, and it was with her seraph-based help that we'd found this small town in the middle of the cornfields.

I'd only actually *seen* Grace the few times I'd dissociated from my amulet—and almost killed myself for good, incidentally. Though tiny, she'd been beautiful, with a face too bright to look at. Most times, she appeared as a haze of glowing light, sort of like the spots you sometimes get in photographs. That was exactly how she showed up on film, and it was the only way a normal human would know she was around. I could hear her. My reapers could, too, but humans could not. Lucky them.

"There once was a girl timekeeper," Grace sang cheerfully as she dropped down to me, bored with playing in the echoes at the ceiling, "who didn't agree with her reaper. So she fought the good fight, thinking choice just might, get the bad guy to think a bit deeper."

"Thanks, Grace," I said wryly.

She brightened, her giggle sounding like falling water. Grace liked her new job of messenger, which she had gained when I first gave her a name. I'd granted her the promotion accidentally, not knowing that names had that much power in the angelic realm. I think the seraphs assigned her to me as punishment, but I'd have it no other way, limericks or not.

"What's with the reapers?" she asked, going invisible when she landed on the top of the trash can beside me. When her wings stopped, she quit glowing.

"You make a dark reaper and a former light reaper work together and see if they don't have issues," I said, sighing as I leaned against the directory and waited. My hand went around my amulet and, in my mind, I reached out to the divine to warp the light around the black stone. Like magic—which it sort of was—the river-smooth stone vanished even though its weight was still heavy in my palm. Making my amulet disappear was one of the first things Nakita had taught me. Someday, I'd be able to make it look like something else, but for now, this was all I could manage.

Grace's wings blurred into sight at my show of "skill," then vanished. "At least they're talking."

"They aren't talking; they're arguing," I said. This was going to be harder than I thought if they were going to "discuss" everything to death. We were here; it was time to start looking for the mark.

"You didn't think changing heaven and earth was going to be easy, did you?" Grace asked, and I frowned.

"It'd be easier if I could flash forward in the time lines and see the future," I complained.

"Give it a chance," Grace said dryly. "You severely damaged your amulet when you dissociated from it."

I winced at the accusation in her tone. She'd told me not to do it, and I'd ignored her. Having done so had saved me, but until my amulet fixed itself, it would be the seraphs who'd be reading the time lines and sending out my dark reapers to kill people.

Seraphs reading the time lines was an imperfect proposition in itself. They could do it, but they had a hard time separating past from future, which was one reason why timekeepers were human. Human timekeepers—which, in this case, would be me—also allowed flexibility over the millennia, sort of giving heaven a way to adapt as perfectly imperfect humans changed their relationship with life, the universe, and everything.

Scythings were taking place that I didn't know about, and it bothered me. The seraphs knew I wanted to change things, and I couldn't help but feel as if I'd been given this scything as a trial. If I couldn't get this guy to see a new choice and make a different decision, how could I hope to get my dark reapers to?

Seeing me depressed, Grace hovered closer. "Don't worry," she soothed. "It won't be long before you're reading the time lines. I think you're already doing so unconsciously. Your instinct to stop at the mall was a good one. I didn't know he was here."

"Is he?" I asked, and she brightened, rising up as Barnabas and Nakita finally came to some agreement and headed our way. Maybe she was right. There *had* been a faint tickling through my mind as we'd flown over the mall, sort of like the feeling of someone watching me. When I'd mentioned it to Barnabas, he had immediately angled for the parking lot. It had given me a boost of confidence, but now, as I looked over the place, I wondered if it had been a true feeling or simply wanting to get my feet back on the earth. The mall didn't look very promising.

It was Monday, so there weren't many people, mostly moms dragging their kids from store to store for school clothes, or kids dragging their moms for the same thing. By an earring cart, a couple of girls were eyeing me. I scuffed my yellow sneakers on the tile, feeling like I fit right in with my punky hair with the purple tips.

"Do you think Josh is okay?" I asked Grace as I fussed with

my short-sleeved, red-and-black-checked shirt. If I'd known that I was going on a reap prevention this morning, I might have worn something a little flashier.

"He'll be fine," Grace said as Barnabas came to a halt before us. Nakita's steps were precise and sure, but upon seeing his slouch she lost some of her upright posture, still trying to fit in as she eyed the girls at the kiosk.

"So, Grace," Barnabas said bluntly, "you sure the seraphs couldn't give you anything more about this mark?"

I sighed. Mark. That was what reapers called potential victims. As in "he won't be anything but a mark on a tombstone."

Nakita smirked, tossing her hair back and smiling at the round haze that was Grace. The original message that had gotten us out of school and out here had been only for her, but Barnabas had listened in. "What's the matter, Barnabas? Not enough information for you? I thought you were good at this."

It was positively catty, and as Barnabas and Nakita started right back up again, I sent my gaze roving. A group of guys by the magazine store had noticed us, or Nakita, rather, her midriff showing in flashes as she lectured Barnabas about seraph supremacy. Spinning on a heel, I walked away from their argument to sit at one of the empty tables. The food court felt right, but I couldn't do this by feel. I had to know.

Immediately their argument switched to who was ticking me off the most, and I heard them start to follow. Grace was favoring them with one of her limericks about "the reapers did fight, with all of their might, till their keeper did leave them behind." Honestly, I was about to. They weren't helping at all.

Finding a table that was sort of clean, I dragged out a chair to sit with my back to the doors. Silent at last, the two reapers took their places on either side of me. Nakita set her empty purse on her lap, nervously fingering her amulet as she watched the girls at the earring kiosk. Her expression was worried—not because of my mood, but because the girls were Gothed to the max in black and lace and she was wearing a red shirt. Barnabas was sullen as he slouched in his faded tee, looking good anyway with his curly hair all over the place.

"Grace," I asked, wondering how I'd become the cool head in this circle. "What exactly did the seraphs tell you?"

This time the reapers stayed quiet, and the messenger angel dropped down to the table, her haze vanishing as she came to a rest.

"Not much," Grace said, her ethereal voice seeming to insert itself in my mind. "Seraphs aren't very good at giving physical descriptions. Apart from the town's location, I know he's good with computers."

Leaning back in the plastic chair, I mentally crossed off the guy at the magazine kiosk reading *Guns & Ammo.*

"The seraphs never said he was a computer geek," Barnabas said dryly.

Nakita bristled. Her hand dropped from her amulet, and my eyebrows rose as I saw that the gray stone had shifted to a Gothic cross. "The seraphs foretold a computer virus being released into a school as a prank," she said to me as she glared at him. "I'd say that would make him good with computers. It's when it gets into the local teaching hospital that people start to die. The seraphs say he finds so much pleasure in the anonymous notoriety that he goes on to do more of the same, intentionally harming people the rest of his life. So you can see why it is in everyone's best interests, *Barney*, to take his soul early, before it's so sullied and turned that he won't ask for redemption."

Gritting his teeth, Barnabas stayed quiet, and I shifted nervously on the chair. Funny how she could make death sound like a good thing.

My spider sense had stopped tingling, and I put my elbows on the table, thinking that this was as about as productive as the study hall I was currently skipping. I'd be willing to bet the guy in the Harley shirt striding through the mall with a girl talking on a phone beside him was out. I needed to find someone with a pocket protector.

"Computer geek," I murmured, squinting as I looked up at the bright windows in the ceiling. I supposed I should be grateful for whatever information the seraphs could give, but, frustrated, I dropped my head onto the table. It hit with a thump, cold against my forehead.

Barnabas put a comforting hand on my shoulder. "Madison, it's okay," he said, making me feel even worse. "We're trying to find this guy incredibly early. The time lines are harder to read the farther out they are from the present. Even Ron is incapable of giving a description before he flashes forward, and that's usually just hours before the mark makes his fatal choice, not an entire day. We're relying on angelic interpretations of what might happen, so relax."

I pulled my head up, still staring at the table. The light timekeeper was not my favorite person these days, but I felt better that Ron was likely unaware we were out here trying to save this guy. Once he knew, it would make things more difficult.

"Madison, you're doing fine! You got us here, didn't you?" Barnabas said, his hand falling away. "I can feel that the mark is here, too. Your instincts are good. We'll find him."

Looking up, I read first his hope, then Nakita's doubt. On the table, Grace was silent, listening. "In time?" I asked. "Before Ron flashes forward and sends someone to stop us? I don't think a light reaper will believe I'm trying to save this guy with Nakita standing beside me, ready to kill him if I can't make him change his mind. Would you?"

Barnabas darted a glance at Nakita, and her grip on her red purse tightened. "Sure I would," he said, but he was lying. "Madison, don't worry. We'll find him. It's just first-prevention jitters."

"It's a reap," Nakita said, looking at her black nails, and then at the Goths. "Not a reap prevention."

"It's whatever Madison makes it," Barnabas shot back, his face turning red.

"Well, I gotta go!" Grace said, the soft glow that was her wings rising up and sending the scent of strawberries to me. "I was told to get you here, then back off."

"You're leaving?" I asked, worried, but then something in Grace's words caught my attention. "Back off?" I repeated, and her glow above the table turned almost a sickly green. "Not leave? Darn it, Grace, are you spying on us?"

Barnabas sat up in concern, and a high-pitched groan came from Grace. "Don't be mad!" she exclaimed. "The seraphs are confused, and they want some reassurance that changing a mark's path is even possible. That's why you *got* this reap, Madison. There's always a shift in policy when a new timekeeper takes over, but there's never been one as big as what you want. They don't think a reaper can open a human's mind to choosing a different path while remaining anonymous, especially if it takes both light and dark reapers working together to do it. If Barnabas and Nakita can't do this with you helping them, how are they expected to do it together when you're not with them?"

I'm helping Barnabas and Nakita? I thought, confused. All I'd been thinking about was how I was going to save this guy, not set a precedent for others to follow. But even I had to concede that Ron didn't handle reaps himself but sent his light reapers out and moved on to the next soul.

"Together?" I questioned, glancing at Barnabas and Nakita, both of them wearing sick looks. "Why would it take them both?"

"Because if the light reaper fails to effect a change, the seraphs want a dark reaper there to scythe the sucker," the guardian angel said cheerfully. "And I'm not spying! I'm evaluating!"

"It's the same difference!" I exclaimed, then hunched into my seat when the guy reading the magazine looked up.

"Well, it's not like you really want the job," Grace snapped. "How much unconditional support are the seraphs supposed to put behind your ideas if you're going to give up the position as soon as you find your real body and turn living again?"

Nakita's expression froze, fear a shadow in the back of her eyes.

Oh, crap. The hum of Grace's wings seemed to grow louder. Nakita wouldn't look away from me. It was as if I'd already abandoned her—me, the person who had accidentally damaged her perfect angel wisdom with a human's understanding of death. She didn't fit in anymore with her dark brethren, and I was possibly the only one who might be able to help her understand why, seeing as it was my memories and fears that had changed her.

"Well, maybe if they'd get behind my ideas a little more, I might keep the job after I find my body," I said in a loud whisper. It wasn't the first time I'd considered keeping it once I found my body. Timekeepers didn't have to be dead—actually, I think I was the first one who was. But I wouldn't stay the head of a system that I didn't believe in. Either they let me do things my way, or I was out of here.

"I don't believe in ultimate fate, and I won't send dark reapers out to cull souls because people are ignorant of choice," I said, knowing that through her, my words would be heard. "If the seraphs can't meet me halfway, then I'm not going to do this, dead or alive."

I was arguing with heaven, but I didn't care. Grace was silent; then the haze of her brightened. "I don't know why you want to be alive anyway," she muttered, apparently willing to concede the point. "It's messy. I mean, you leak liquids from every orifice and can't stay awake."

"Yeah, and we eat, too," I said sourly. "Do you know how long it's been since food tasted good?" It was a good thing I didn't need to, or I would have starved by now.

She made a tiny harrumph, and a new urgency layered over me like a second skin. Swell. Not only did I have to save some guy's life, but I had to get Barnabas and Nakita to work together in the process? Great. Just freaking great.

"You didn't think it was going to be easy, did you?" Grace said from the middle of the table, her glow shifting wildly through the spectrum before she shot straight up like a reverse falling star and slipped right out through the high skylights. We appeared to be alone, but I'd bet she was watching.

No one said anything, and I looked from Barnabas to Nakita, who was ignoring me, her expression grim. "I'm going to get a shake," I said suddenly, not at all hungry of course but needing the excuse to get away from them for a moment. "You guys want anything?"

I didn't wait for an answer, and standing up, I almost ran into a chair someone had left out. Catching my balance against it, I stopped short and carefully set it under a table, trying to make it look like I'd meant to do it. Striding over to the restaurants, I swear I thought I heard Grace giggle.

I'd ditched school with high expectations, but now I was feeling totally inadequate. It wasn't an unfamiliar emotion, but this was the first time someone's life was in the balance. Picking a restaurant without a line, I set my hands on the counter and stared up at the menu, not really seeing it. I had the cash my dad had given me for lunch, not that I ever ate lunch anymore. Crap, I had to text him that I might be late after school today.

"You going to read it, or order from it?" said a voice right in front of me, and I jerked, bringing my attention down to find a guy about my age in a lame-looking apron with a chicken on it, boldly stating, THE CHICKEN COOP, ONE GOOD CLUCK. A paper hat tried to contain his sandy blond hair, but failed. He had a nice face, and he smiled as he saw my embarrassment. His name tag said ACE. My thoughts zinged to Josh, and I felt a moment of guilt that he had been left at school.

"Uh, can I have a vanilla shake? Small," I said, since I wasn't really going to drink it, and he beeped it up.

"Anything for your friends?"

I turned to see Nakita with one hand on her purse, watching me with a lost look on her face. Barnabas had his head thrown back, staring at the ceiling as if he were bored. At least they weren't fighting. "You've been watching me?" I asked, tilting my head to look coy. Stupid, but coy.

Ace plucked a cup a size larger than I'd ordered and smiled. "Nice move with the chair. Almost looked like you meant to do that."

I rolled my eyes, cursing Grace for leaving it there for me. "Yeah," I said, shifting from foot to foot, terribly conscious of my hair. I hadn't seen anyone here with purple hair except for the pierced goddess working at Hot Topic.

Ace was silent, his back to me as he filled up the cup. There was only one other guy working in the back room, cleaning the ovens. It was too early for lunch. "So, when does school start for you?" I asked, needing to say something.

Ace turned around, eyeing me slyly as he snapped a top on the shake. "Tomorrow. I wasn't even supposed to be here this morning, and then they called. Man, I could've killed my mom." He slid the drink to me. "I had my day already planned. Surfing the web and eating cheese puffs. That's the last time I let my mom get the phone and answer for me."

"I work part-time at a flower shop, and I hate it when my dad does that."

Ace adjusted his hat, grimacing. "If I'm at work, she knows where I am," he said sourly. "She's always checking up on me like I'm a kid. She works at the hospital, so she sees everything that comes in through the emergency room and thinks I'm going to get in an accident."

My mind flitted back to waking up in my local morgue, dead from a car crash. My heart began thumping. I didn't think it was the memory of me dying, though. A tingling was rising through my aura as a thought evolved in my mind. *His mom works at the hospital? Can it be this easy? Maybe that's what Barnabas meant about my instincts being good.* "I hear you," I said, glancing at Barnabas and Nakita, but they were staring at me, oblivious.

"So now everything I want to do today, I do tomorrow," Ace said, shrugging.

I jerked myself back from my thoughts. "You said you have school tomorrow."

"I said school starts tomorrow. I didn't say I was going to be there."

Ooh, a little rebel, are we? I took a straw, tearing it open and jamming it into the shake. "You ditching your first day of school?" I asked, pretending to take a sip of my shake.

"Something like that," he said, smiling right back. "I got more important stuff to do."

"Like what?" I said, smiling like the cool girls at my old school had taught me before I ditched them.

Ace laughed, flattered on some level. "Music. Shoe and me, we get music."

He tossed his attention briefly to the black-haired guy in the back, and I felt a drop of disappointment. "You're in a band?" I asked. Crap, it had been nothing after all.

"No, not *make* it. We *get* it. Before it's released."

The stress he'd put on his words pulled me back. "You lift it?" I asked, eyes widening. If he could hack a music site, a hospital computer would be nothing.

Excited, I edged forward. The move was not lost on Ace, and he leaned across the counter, hitting the sale button and closing the drawer almost before it had opened. "Last week," he whispered, his eyes glinting, "Shoe got into a major record label's site and lifted a track of Coldplay's music not out until next spring."

I shivered, my aura seeming to chime. He could break into secure sites. "Really? Can I hear it?"

Ace drew back, slyly standing behind the counter as if he were king of the world. "Shoe and I don't let anyone listen. Not until we're done. I gotta put the cover art on the disc. Then you can *buy* it."

My breath huffed out of me. Feigning disbelief, I cocked my hip. "Okay, I get it," I said in a bored tone. "Whatever."

But Ace laughed. "You don't believe me?" Turning to the back, he shouted, "Shoe! Tell her the name of Coldplay's newest album."

The boy in the back pulled himself out of the oven he had been cleaning. There was grease smudged on his shoulder and he looked mad. "What the hell is wrong with you, Ace?" he exclaimed. "You're going to get us caught!"

"Dude!" Ace said, holding his hands up in mock surrender. "Cool your stick, man. She's not going to say anything."

Shoe threw the rag he'd been using at Ace, but it fell far short. "You don't even know who she is!" he yelled, and a side door to the kitchen banged open and a short man wearing a shirt a size too small for him came out. Manager. I could tell even before I saw his lame brown shoes with the tiny brown laces.

"Mitch, we got a problem here?" he asked, and Shoe turned to him, still ticked.

"No!" he shouted. Taking the oven cleaner, he sprayed it wildly on the front of the next oven.

"Chill, dude!" Ace said. "It's not a big deal!" He was almost laughing, and it only made Shoe angrier, his motions becoming fast and erratic.

The manager saw it, too, and he came closer. "Relax," the man said, trying to look as if he were in charge. "I've put up with your temper all summer."

Shoe turned. "Yeah? Well, I quit!" he shouted, slamming the oven cleaner down. "I don't need this crap!"

"No, you're fired!" the man said, and Ace started to laugh, looking at the food court to see who was watching. "Clock out, and don't come back. I'll mail you your last check! And don't bother asking for a reference."

"You can keep your lousy money," Shoe muttered, and I watched in alarm as Shoe took off his apron and threw it down in disgust. Turning to Ace, who clearly thought it was all a big joke, Shoe said, "You're a freaking loser, Ace. You know that? You're so stupid you can't even keep your mouth shut. We're done. Got it? You're on your own."

Ace's face colored, anger etching his features in an instant. "Yeah?" he said loudly. "Well, you can go screw a rat, asshole!" Ace's sudden shift to anger felt wrong, and I gripped my shake tighter, trying to figure it out.

My mouth fell open, and I dropped back a step. The entire food court was watching now.

"Out!" the manager shouted, his round face turning red. "Both of you!"

"I didn't even want to come in today, you tub of lard," Ace said under his breath, but I knew the manager heard him, because he started to huff as if he were out of breath.

Shaking with anger, the manager pointed at the mall's doors. "Get out!"

I scrambled back when Ace put a hand on the counter and vaulted over it. From the rear of the kitchen came the slamming of a heavy door as Shoe stormed off. Snatching his hat from his head, Ace dropped it on the tiled floor. "This job sucks," he said, and he walked away, taking his apron off as he went and letting it fall.

The manager was fuming, and I hesitantly said, "Uh, how much do I owe you?"

He looked up as if noticing me for the first time, his thoughts clearly on Ace and Shoe. "Nothing. It's free," he said. "I'm sorry you had to see that. He's been smart-mouthing me all summer. I should have fired him the third day he was here."

"Sorry," I said, not knowing why I was apologizing. Feeling weird, I turned and went back to Nakita and Barnabas. Eyes down, I slid into my seat and took a sip of shake.

Barnabas cleared his throat. "What was all that about?"

The ugliness washed from me, and I looked up, smiling at Nakita, then Barnabas. "I found our mark. It's Ace."

Nakita fingered her amulet as if she wanted to follow him out and scythe him in the parking lot. I was starting to understand why the seraphs believed light and dark reapers couldn't work together. Getting Nakita to hold off until we'd given Ace a chance to change his ways wasn't going to be easy. "Are you sure?" she asked, eyes alight and eager.

I nodded, sharing her enthusiasm if not the reason behind it. I could do this. I'd just relaxed as Barnabas had said, and let my intuition tell me. "Pretty sure," I said. "Ace is good with computers and doesn't mind breaking the law. He says school starts tomorrow, but that he's ditching it. His mom works at the hospital and has such a tight leash on him that he's probably ready to do anything to make her mad." I watched Ace walk through the parking lot, all the while thinking about my dad and how closely he watched me. No longer in his apron, Ace looked kind of rough in a pair of faded jeans and a black T-shirt.

"Let's go," I said when Ace angrily smacked a car at random.

"I've got to talk to him."

We stood up as one, but Barnabas was hesitant. "I don't know," he said as we started after him. "It sounded like Shoe was the computer guy."

I turned to him, the shake cold in my grip. "You heard that?"

"Everyone heard that," Nakita said, tossing her hair. Her purse slung over her shoulder, she walked to the doors as if she were a runway model.

Doubt hit me, and my fast pace slowed.

"Shoe lost his temper first," Barnabas said. "And if he's the one who hacked the system, then he's the one who can make the virus, not the guy who does the cover art."

I frowned as we hit the doors and came out into the early afternoon sun. Past the yellow line in the employee parking area, Ace was standing next to a sporty car and arguing with Shoe. Biting my lip, I thought of Barnabas's thousand-year-plus experience at this compared to my intuition. It was probably Shoe, but I didn't want to lose sight of Ace. The memory of how quickly his mood shifted wouldn't leave me. Something was wrong there.

"Okay," I said hesitantly as we started to move forward again. "Barnabas, if you think it's Shoe, you should follow him. Nakita and I will stick with Ace and learn what we can." *And it will keep you and Nakita apart, too.*

Nakita made a pleased sound, clearly glad to be taking

action. "I should be the one to follow Shoe, not Barnabas," she said firmly. "That way, if he tries to put the virus in a computer, I'll be there to kill him."

I stopped short, and she went two steps before halting. My gaze went to Barnabas, and he made a helpless expression. "Um, Nakita, I thought you'd come with me."

The reaper was clueless about many things, but she wasn't stupid. A soft blush marred her face, and she went stiff, her black toenails shining in the sun. "You're trying to keep me away from Shoe."

I was trying to keep her away from Barnabas, too. I took a breath to protest, then let it out. "Yeah, but come with me anyway. Ace likes pretty girls. He'll tell you anything." Nakita squinted at me, and I added, "Come on. Help me out here. Ron can't possibly know we're out of Three Rivers yet, so we've got tons of time."

"She *is* your boss," Barnabas muttered, and Nakita frowned.

"Okay," she said, capitulating, "but if Shoe does anything, promise you'll call me, Barnabas."

"You want me to *call* you?" Barnabas said, thumbs in his jeans pockets and the wind shifting his T-shirt. "How? You're a dark reaper, and I'm light. Our resonances are too far apart for our amulets to allow it."

Nakita smiled, changing her amulet from the Gothic cross back to its normal flat stone cradled in a basket of silver wire. "You're not as light as you think, reaper. Looked at your aura lately? You've gone neutral. I bet we can talk through our amulets if we try. You're going dark. Dude."

Barnabas's expression became horrified, and he looked down at his own amulet. Taking Nakita's arm, I pushed her into motion before Ace drove away. I knew Barnabas wasn't happy about losing his light-reaper status, but she didn't have to torment him about it. Since leaving Ron and the light reapers, he was considered a grim reaper, a group of vigilante angels scorned by light and dark reapers alike for their wont to kill without reason. If there was a plague, grim reapers were there. A disaster had them wading into the bodies like they were surf. War was their play yard. It wouldn't be until Barnabas's amulet color shifted closer to mine that he might be considered respectable again, but since he'd then be a dark reaper who didn't believe in fate, he wasn't truly going to fit in. Heaven probably wouldn't let him back, either.

"I'll get you guys some phones next time I'm in the mall," I said sourly. But if I knew how to use my friggin' amulet to talk silently with them, then I wouldn't need to.

"Ace!" I shouted, the hard pavement under my feet sending jolts through me as I ran for his truck. "Wait up!"

Nakita, apparently, saw no reason to run, and she sedately followed somewhere behind me, handbag at her side and matching sandals clicking away. Barnabas was heading off in the opposite direction, probably seeking a quiet place to wait and take wing to follow Shoe. Shoe's back was hunched as he stomped to a lonely sports car parked by itself in a spot of shade.

Hearing my voice, Ace leaned against his truck and put his thumbs in his pockets. I slowed, not even breathing heavily. Okay, so maybe there were some benefits to this whole being-dead thing. Nakita caught up with me, and I slowed even more. "He's angry," she said simply as we matched paces. "Are you sure he'll tell us anything?"

"Yeah, well, you can be mad at your friends," I said, remembering how I'd been angry with Wendy, my best friend in Florida, where I'd lived before I moved to Three Rivers. Most of our arguments had stemmed from my trying to get us into the cool crowd, but Wendy was too independent. Even when we fought, though, we remained friends.

"How can you be angry and like someone at the same time?" Nakita asked.

I watched Shoe get in his car and start it up, revving the engine hard. "You just do. You like Barnabas, don't you? Even when you argue?"

"No," she said immediately, then hesitated. "He's smarter than I thought he was. Thinking that he might be right and I might be wrong makes me angry."

"Same thing here," I said, indicating Ace, who was now pushing up from the truck and brushing a hand across his wrinkled T-shirt.

She fingered her amulet and asked, "Who's right?"

I smiled at Ace and said, "It doesn't matter."

She sighed. "I don't understand."

"It's a friendship thing." Shifting my smile brighter, I scuffed to a halt, turning the popular-girl charm on full. It usually got me my way with strangers, so the time I'd spent trying to get in with the cool girls hadn't been a total loss. I guess.

But my smile faded when Ace almost barked, "What do you want?"

Nakita reached for her amulet, and I "accidentally" came down on her foot. "Uh, nothing," I said as she shoved me off her, but I was already rocking back. "I wanted to say I'm sorry I got you fired. It was kind of my fault."

I gave him a sad, big-eyed look, and sure enough, he shifted from P.O.'ed to accommodating. Ah, the power of a pretty face. Too bad he was looking at Nakita's and not mine. But she was an angel. Why was I even trying to compete?

"It wasn't your fault," he said, his voice softening. "Shoe's an ass." A flash of anger reddened his face, and he shouted after Shoe's car, "Dumb ass!"

"Can I scythe him, too? Just for the fun of it?" Nakita asked, and Ace turned, shocked.

"Stop it," I muttered, but he'd heard.

"What did you say?"

I licked my lips, scrambling for words. "So you like music?" I blurted, and he turned back to me.

As he glanced from me to Nakita, I could almost see his thoughts realign, wondering if he had a chance with her. Sure, that was likely. Not.

"Yep," he said, still looking at her, and she suddenly smiled back and giggled like Amy, my earthly nemesis at school in designer sandals. Hearing that noise come out of her shocked the b-juice out of me, and I wasn't surprised when Ace added, "I don't have anything to do now. You want to hear some?"

"Absolutely!" I said enthusiastically, and he shifted away

from the front door, hitting his shoulder on the side mirror and trying not to lose his cool.

"Get in," he said, opening the door. "I live twenty minutes from here. You can hear the new stuff."

For a moment, I looked in at the long bench seat, remembering the last time I got into a stranger's car. I'd ended up at the bottom of a ravine, dead. *Well, you can't kill someone twice,* I thought. Besides, Nakita was with me. Stepping carefully to avoid the CDs tossed everywhere, I got in, sliding to the far door. The truck was old, with cracked vinyl seats and a dusty, sun-faded dash. The CD cases made bright flashes when the light caught them, and I snatched one out from under Nakita before she sat right on it. It was clearly home-burned, with an art decal on one side. Josh had an old truck, too, but he at least kept his clean. I had a thought to text him and see how he was doing, but texting a guy in front of Ace probably wasn't the best way to convince him to show me his illegal downloads.

"Is this your work?" I asked as Ace got in, slamming his door twice to make it latch. Just from looking at their cars, I could tell there was a big discrepancy between Ace and Shoe, and I wondered if that was where some of the anger was coming from. Jealousy, maybe.

"Shoe's," he said tersely.

"No, I mean the artwork," I added, and his tight jaw relaxed as he cranked the key and the engine started. "I like it."

Music blared, heavy on the percussion, and the singer

screaming so you couldn't understand what he was saying. "Thanks," he said as he turned the music down so we could hear him. "My mom thinks I could get a scholarship, but what's the point? It's not like I can make a living with squiggles."

I thought of my own dream of making a living with my photography, and a sigh of understanding slipped from me. "Maybe," I said hesitantly. "But it's easier to find a way to make money at something you love than to learn to love a job that you can make money at."

He didn't say anything, and feeling Nakita's eyes on me, I rolled the window down. Jeez, it was a crank, and it was stiff, like it hadn't been down in a year. Slowly the still air was replaced by new as we headed for the exit, pulling out to go the same way Shoe had. There had been a small town east of here when we'd flown in, right in the middle of cornfields.

Ace bobbed his head in time with the music, glancing at Nakita to see how she liked it.

My attention dropped to the CD I was holding, and I put it on the dash, fingering another one decorated with similar artwork. It was all swirls and stark, bright colors, making me think of Celtic knot work.

"This is good," I said as I looked at the handful of discs within my easy reach. "The artwork, I mean. You should talk to your art teacher. I bet she knows of a scholarship."

"People like them don't help people like me," Ace said, his mood tarnishing. "Besides, college . . . that's not for me."

My eyebrows rose. *People like him?*

"That's mine, too," he said, and I followed his pointing finger to the overpass we were going under. It was covered in graffiti with the same swirls and angles. Archetype symbols were worked into it everywhere, making it look like sort of a mix between a tattoo and a stained-glass window.

"Wow," I said, turning in the seat to find that the other side of the overpass was decorated as well. "That's beautiful."

Ace smiled a bad-boy smile and tapped his fingers in time with the drums. "Almost got caught the last night I worked on it. They were waiting for me. Look at the water tower."

Nakita made a strangled sound, and I followed her gaze to the bulbous thing rising high over the cornfields. My mouth dropped open, and I stared.

"You like it?" Ace asked, and I nodded, too shocked to do more.

"It looks like a black wing!" Nakita whispered, and I nodded again. Wrapped around the water tower was a black-and-white crow, looking as if it were melting into a dripping puddle of goo. It looked exactly like a black wing might look to the living, sort of a mix of sophisticated graffiti and Native American petroglyphs. Black wings were unintelligent scavengers of the soul world, showing up at a reaping in hopes of snitching a bit of unattended soul. I hated them, and they gave me the creeps. Both light and dark reapers used them to help zero in on a target, even as loathsome as they were.

"I've made that my trademark," Ace was saying, and I dragged my attention back to him.

"The crows?" I said, stifling a shiver. "Where did you get the idea to make them melt like that?"

His jaw clenched. "Shoe."

Back to Shoe. It looked like Barnabas was right: Shoe was our target, not Ace.

Ace took one hand off the wheel and looked at Nakita. "You don't talk much."

"I don't see the point when actions are more convincing," she said stiffly, behaving completely at odds to that giggle earlier.

Nodding his head like she'd said something wise, Ace said, "Me too."

I had to get back to Shoe. Barnabas had been right. "Hey, I'm sorry about your friend," I said hesitantly, trying to turn the conversation to him.

Ace made a huff of sound. "He's an ass. I've known him since third grade, and he's always been an ass. Nothing here is ever good enough for him. He's always after the big city and a 'better life.' What's wrong with just staying here and being normal?"

"He's the hacker?" I asked. "You do the artwork, and he gets the stuff?"

Ace stared straight ahead, his speed never changing. "Yup," he said sarcastically. "I'm just the guy who makes it look cool. He's going off to college at the end of this year. Between filling out applications and prepping for the skills test, I only see him at work."

Ohhh, he's jealous. Feeling ditched. It might be the wrong time, but we were going to run out of cornfields eventually. I didn't want to spend the day with Ace when it was Shoe who was in danger. "Uh, do you think you could take us to Shoe's house?" I asked, and Ace leaned forward past Nakita to see me.

"You've got to be kidding," Ace said in disgust. "This is to get to him, isn't it? You girls are all the same. You see a fancy car and you think I'm dirt."

"No!" I exclaimed, my pulse jumping into play. Sensing it, Nakita looked at me. "Ace, Shoe is in danger," I said, and seeing his anger, I blurted, "I know all about the virus he wants to upload to the school. It's going to kill people."

The truck swerved and Ace looked at me, shocked.

"Watch the road!" I shouted as I remembered going into the ravine. My hand slammed against the dash. But he wasn't listening to me.

"Computer viruses don't kill people," he said, angry. "How did you find out about it? Did he tell you? Did Shoe tell you, and then get mad at me for telling you about some stupid music we lifted?"

His voice hurt my ears, and I glanced from him to the road, glad no one was coming. "He didn't tell me," I said. "It's my job to know stuff."

Ace laughed, but I breathed easier when he looked back at

the road. Nakita sat still between us, fingering her amulet and staying out of it, but her frown told me she thought I was making a mistake.

"It's your job, huh? And who are you, silent girl? Her muscle?"

Nakita dropped her hand to steady her little purse on her knees. "Yes."

He laughed bitterly again, shaking his head as he muttered, "I'm a crazy-chick magnet. Crazy-freaking-chick magnet."

A flush of anger lit through me. "I don't care if you believe me or not," I said sharply, "but that virus is going to escape the school and get into the hospital. People are going to die." I shifted my tone, pleading. "You've got to help me convince Shoe not to do it. He won't listen to me, but you're his friend."

Ace looked at me, his eyes holding a heady anger. "Screw you," he said suddenly. "And screw Shoe. Why should I give a crap about him?"

Frustrated, I let go of the dash. Shoe was going to college, and Ace wasn't. He was afraid he wasn't good enough to keep up, and it was easier to hate Shoe than try and maybe fail.

"We're not going to Shoe's?" Nakita asked.

"I'd sooner go to hell," Ace said, and Nakita moved.

"Hey!" Ace shouted as Nakita suddenly turned in her seat and grabbed his shirt.

"You are not going to hell. You are going to take us to Shoe's house," she demanded, and the truck swerved.

"Nakita! Let go!" I shouted as we crossed the yellow line, then swerved back, our tires going right off the road.

"Let go of me, you crazy chick!" Ace shouted, one wheel still off the road as we continued at a fast sixty miles an hour. Slowly he brought us back on the pavement, and only after all four wheels were on the road did he use his brakes and we lurched to a stop.

"Get out!" Ace was shouting. "Get out of my truck, you freaks!"

I was more than ready to, and I shoved the door open and slid onto the hot pavement. I was shaking, sick almost, at the reminder of the car accident that had killed me.

"I told you to take us to Shoe," Nakita said from inside the truck.

"And I told you to get out!" Her purse sailed into the air, landing by my feet. "I've never hit a girl, but you're pushing it, babe. Why is it that the sexy ones are all nuts?"

Babe? Had he really called her babe?

Nakita was ready to lose it, and I reached in to pull on her arm. "Come on, let's go."

I yanked her out right as Ace hit the gas, accelerating with his tires hiccuping on the pavement. The door wasn't even shut.

"Crazy chicks!" he shouted, leaving a pall of oil smoke and the fading sound of his engine.

Nakita stood beside me, shaking in anger. "I am not crazy," she said as she scooped up her empty little red purse, and I silently agreed with her. The sound of Ace's truck quickly faded, and I looked up and down the deserted road, wondering where Barnabas was.

"That didn't work out the way I wanted," I said, starting to walk in the direction Ace had gone. The town couldn't be too far ahead.

Nakita fixed her sandal, then started to follow, *click*, *click*, *click* on the hot pavement. "You told him too much. Marks never believe. That's why we scythe them."

There was a silent accusation in her tone that I was being stupid even to try to change several thousand years of tradition. Pensive, I watched the straight rows of tall corn slowly shift as we walked. At least Barnabas was watching the right person.

"Shouldn't we find Barnabas?" Nakita asked, looking unsure at my continued silence. "I tried calling him when I was in Ace's truck and couldn't reach him. He's not dark enough yet. You might be able to get a hold of him, though."

"Me?" I squawked, embarrassed even though she already knew about the weeks of failure when Barnabas and I had sat on my roof and tried. "My amulet is too far from his, too. Light reaper, dark timekeeper . . . You know," I said, glad I had my phone. If worse came to worst, I'd call my dad and tell him I was doing something with Josh. He'd cover for me. *I shouldn't have told Ace all that. No wonder he thinks we're nuts. I'd think we were nuts.*

Nakita's steps became silent as she walked straight down the middle of the road, following the broken yellow line. "Barnabas's amulet resonance was the red of a light reaper the last time you tried," she said, and I glanced over at her, thinking we looked quite the pair. "It's shifted to a grim reaper's neutral green since then. I can't reach him, but your timekeeper amulet is more fluid than mine, and he's the one you've been practicing with. I can hear his amulet resonating in the ether, so he hasn't shielded himself yet. I can carry you, but it would be easier to find Barnabas if we knew exactly where he was."

I sighed, my hand going up to touch my amulet. Every time I tried to use it, either nothing happened or I made a mistake.

"What will you lose by trying?" Nakita coaxed. "Barnabas should know what happened. For all his insufferable know-it-all attitude, he's part of our . . . team."

She had said that last word like it tasted bad, and a slight smile brightened my mood. She was trying. "Okay," I said agreeably, "but if I can't reach him, we'll find him by air."

She nodded, and I felt a quiver of anticipation. It would be great if I could do this. My amulet was the same deep, glittery black that it had been since I claimed it, but Barnabas's *had* shifted down the spectrum. Nakita was right: It just might be possible.

Excited, I turned to the tall cornfields, then the empty road—listening to the sound of the wind. Either nothing would happen, or I'd make it work. It wasn't as if I didn't know the theory inside and out after countless nights on my roof trying.

Stopping, I sat right down on the edge of the road, shifting until the pebbles didn't grind into my ankles.

Nakita understandably stared at me.

"I'm not good at it," I explained, embarrassed. "I need to sit down." Closing my eyes, I took three slow breaths—my way of inducing a feeling of calm. My shoulders eased, and I exhaled.

In my mind's eye, I tried to imagine my aura. It wasn't really my aura, since I was dead, but the amulet's resonance acted the same way. Because I had the dark timekeeper amulet, my aura or resonance was a violet so dark as to be off the visible spectrum and basically black. Eyes shut, I reached up to hold the glittery black stone cradled in a silver wire and looped around my neck with a simple cord. As long as I had it within twenty feet of me, I had the illusion of a body. If I got too far from it, black wings would sense me and swarm to eat my soul—twenty measly feet between me and utter death. It looked a lot like a reaper amulet, but it was more powerful and yet—as Nakita had said—more flexible. Claiming it from my predecessor hadn't blown my soul to dust like my trying to claim a reaper's amulet would have. Most people didn't even see it unless I pointed it out. I could take it off, but I was reluctant to do so.

The silver wires cradling the stone were warm, but the stone was warmer, as if holding the heat of the sun. All I had to do, in theory, was imagine my thoughts taking on the same color or wavelength as my aura so it could slip free of me. Then I had to hold my thoughts as I shifted the color to match Barnabas's aura so my thoughts could slip through his aura and he could hear it. His resonance was green now. It shouldn't be as hard as trying to shift all the way up the spectrum. Maybe I could do it. Maybe.

I brought Barnabas to mind, his smile, his dark humor, his odd way of looking at the world, the age behind his brown eyes, and how they flashed silver when he touched the divine. *Barnabas*, I thought, shifting my thoughts as "violet" as I could to get them past my aura. *Nakita and I are kind of stuck here on the road.*

A thrill lit through me as I felt my thoughts wing out from me to bounce against the inside of the sphere of air that surrounded the earth. But then, my entire thought seemed to explode in a bright light. Shocked, I opened my eyes and blinked.

"I felt them leave you," Nakita said, smiling. "But they scattered when they diffracted against the sun. You need to modify your thoughts to his aura before they bounce off the atmosphere, not after."

She felt it, I thought, stifling a quiver of anticipation. Barnabas had never said that when we practiced. I shifted awkwardly on the pavement to disguise my shiver, thinking this would look stupid to anyone driving by. Not that we'd seen anyone on the road yet. This was the closest I'd ever gotten to making this work. Nakita had been able to teach me how to bend light around my amulet to hide it, too. Maybe Nakita, for all her awkward inabilities among people, was the better teacher. And wouldn't Barnabas be happy about that?

"Let me try again," I whispered, closing my eyes and calming my thoughts to get them past my aura resonance, and then thinking with a precise narrowness, *Barnabas, we're stuck on the road. Can you find us?*

"Now!" Nakita exclaimed, and I twisted my thought, making the wave wider, more green, perhaps. It hit the curve of the atmosphere and bounced back, being drawn into something as if it belonged. Barnabas, maybe?

Stiffening, I gasped when I got a flash of feeling, like a memory belonging to someone else. It was as if I were seeing from Barnabas's eyes as he sat in some bushes across the street from a nice house, and he jumped as my thought popped into his mind. Then he was gone, and I was surrounded by sand and squinting from the sun. I was wearing a white shirt billowing in the oppressively dry wind. A young man with black eyes sat across from me working on a laptop, his clothes as white and billowy as mine. Someone swore as my thought echoed in his, and I opened my eyes, finding myself back on the road in the middle of the cornfields.

Ohhhh, this can't be good.

Nakita was crouched before me, a hand on my shoulder, concern in her eyes, and her black hair falling about her face. "Madison? Are you all right?"

Squinting, I held out my hand and she took it, backing up to help me stand. I looked down at my sneakers and brushed off my tights. A bad feeling was growing in me, and when she saw my expression, I sensed Nakita's worry shift to alarm.

"How fast can you fly?" I asked, and she stared at me as if I were nuts.

"Why?" she asked, and I looked at the sky, wincing.

"Because I think I just told Ron we're up to something."

Four

Nakita stood beside me in her designer jeans and trendy sandals, her black toenails catching a glint of sun. Her eyes darted from the sky to the rustling fields on both sides of us. Her amulet was blazing a violet that sent purple flashes of light against the darker shadows in the corn. Hair swinging, she spun in a circle, scanning the sky.

"Barnabas, where are you?" she said, and I shivered. Gone was the hesitancy, the awkwardness. She was an avenging angel, and nothing would get past her. "Perhaps we should leave without him. I'm hiding your amulet signature, but if Barnabas can follow the echo of your thought here, then Chronos can, too."

I didn't move, listening to the wind rattle the papery leaves and scanning the heavens and my aura for any prickling of energy. Damn it, if Ron knew we were here, it would make everything more difficult.

"Barnabas," Nakita breathed as she fixed on something I couldn't see, and I had a thought that it was probably the first time she'd been glad to see him.

My own shoulders eased, but I still felt queasy as I remembered being in Ron's head. It had to have been him. If I could reach his thoughts, then he could reach mine. And who was the guy with him? His replacement? My future adversary?

Ron—or Chronos, as he was formally called—was slime. Yes, he believed in choice over fate, as I did. Yes, he sent light reapers out to stop dark reapers from culling souls from bodies too soon, as I would have liked to. If things were different, we'd be working toward the same thing. But he had lied to me about who I was when I'd been killed. He kept from me that I was a timekeeper until it was too late and my body had been hidden away by Kairos, forcing me to accept my dark-timekeeper status in order to stay alive. He had betrayed me and Barnabas both and lied to heaven in his attempt to shift the balance of heavenly power on earth to his favor. And he was supposed to be the good guy.

Nakita's sandals scraped against the pavement, worry etched deep into her brow. "Soon as Barnabas gets here, we leave. Neither of us can stand up to Chronos," she said, visibly upset. "He can stop time."

I edged closer to her, wishing Barnabas had landed already.

He was just a spot of white in the otherwise blue sky. "It's okay," I said, as if trying to convince myself. "Even if Ron does freeze time, he can't kill me."

She turned to me, her eyes shifting silver for an instant as she touched on the divine. "But what if he takes you where I can't follow?"

Swallowing hard, I shrugged. "Why would he? We're just out here standing on a road. Maybe he'll simply send a reaper to check it out." But it was more than that, and we both knew it. Once Ron knew what we were up to, he'd simply slap a guardian angel on Shoe and I'd lose.

I looked up when the light was eclipsed for an instant, only to blind myself when a pair of white wings blinked out the sun. In a gust of air, Barnabas landed before us, his brown eyes shining with delight. "Madison, you did it!" he said, his wings arching up, the tips crossing an instant before they vanished. Striding forward, he exclaimed, "I knew you could. When your thought slipped into mine . . . I am so proud of you!" But then he jerked to a halt upon noticing Nakita's and my worry. "What's wrong?"

Nakita took a firm stance, eyes on the sky again. "Her message echoed into Chronos's mind as well as yours."

"He's probably coming," I said miserably.

"How?" Barnabas said, looking confused. "His resonance isn't anywhere near mine."

Nakita's eyes were darting everywhere. "They are both

timekeepers," she said. "You don't think the seraphs created them such that they could talk if they wanted to?"

"I saw through his eyes," I added.

"Sweet updrafts!" Barnabas cursed. "Are you shielding her?"

"Of course I'm shielding her, you broken feather!" Nakita snapped. "But I'm sure he got a glimpse of where we are before I got my shield in place. You did, didn't you?"

Barnabas grimaced. Taking my elbow, he pulled us off the road, almost into the hissing cornstalks. "Fine. We leave," he said to Nakita. "Let's get out of here before he *does* show up."

Nakita nodded and her amulet blazed as she shrugged her shoulders and her wings appeared. In an instant, I was between two angels, one with light wings, one with dark, both worried. "Why can't I ever do anything right?" I asked, not expecting an answer, but when I got scared, I talked.

Barnabas stretched his wings again—they ran from one edge of the road to the other. "It's not right or wrong," he said, gathering me close to carry me into the air. "You did it, and now you need to learn how to focus. Why do you expect yourself to be perfect the first time? I'd have you try it again right now, but we have to stay shielded from here on out, and a shielded mind is a closed one."

Silent, I leaned back into him, breathing in the smell of sun and feathers. Although he said it was okay, it would still be my fault if Ron figured out we were up to something.

"You did well," he said as his arm slipped around me. "You've worked hard for this skill, and you should be happy."

"Thanks," I said, feeling slightly better as I stepped back onto his feet.

But he didn't move. Actually, nothing was moving—not Barnabas, the wind, or the corn—and I jerked when I felt a nebulous something touch my amulet and claim a portion of it.

Instinct kicked in, and drawing on hours of practice, I brought up my inner sight of my amulet, placing it among the fabric of time.

The "now" was a shimmering line stretching to infinity. On it was my soul sending out thoughts into the future, pulling me along as they fastened me to the future an instant before it became the present. Behind me in my inner sight I could see my past, interweaving heavily with Barnabas, Nakita, and even the bright silver thoughts of Ace. But it wasn't just my thoughts that were attaching my amulet to the present, as was normal. There were someone else's.

Ron, I thought in a panic, wiping a theoretical hand over the fabric of time to destroy his amulet's ties, and only his amulet's ties, to me.

I opened my eyes. . . . The entire process had taken less time than a bubble bursting.

"Barnabas?" I quavered, seeing his arm still around me. I slid from his unmoving grip. Panic slipped between my thought and action. Ron had stopped time. *Son of a puppy.*

Heart pounding, I turned in the absolute stillness of stopped time. There, right in the middle of the road, was Ron.

Ron wasn't a tall man, not much more than my height, which wasn't surprising, since he was born a thousand years ago. I think his height bothered him. His tightly curled graying hair had once been black, and his complexion was dark. His eyes shifted color upon his mood, and I wondered if mine did now, too. He was wearing the same light-colored outfit that I'd seen him in moments ago in my head, sort of Greek-looking. Seeing him standing ten feet away with a shocked expression gave me a flash of satisfaction. Maybe he hadn't expected me to break his hold so easily.

"Stop it," I said as I gripped my amulet. His trying to take my amulet wasn't likely, since he couldn't use it, but it was still hard for me to let go of the warm stone.

Ron squinted down the long road behind me. "Congratulations," he said, "both on breaking my hold on your amulet and learning how to converse silently with it. I know Barnabas didn't teach you. He has the imagination of an earthworm. Did the seraphs? Maybe you could use your inside voice next time? You were shouting."

He was being sarcastic, and I flung a hand out in warning when he took a step forward. Stopping short, he put a hand on his hip to look at me like someone might look at a yapping dog behind a fence. "What are you doing out here? Isn't it a school day?"

"Nothing you need to worry about," I said, backing up to be side by side with Barnabas and Nakita. "Let them go."

He smiled. I remembered when I believed in it. "You don't need to be afraid of me, Madison. I won't hurt you. The seraphs would kill me. You're their next big hope." He shook his head, almost laughing at me.

"There are worse things than being hurt." *And I bet you know all of them*, I thought, wishing I had Barnabas and Nakita to back me. Jeez, it was weird having them silent and unmoving behind me. With a sudden thought, I brought up the nether sight of my mind, searching the fabric of time for the violet glow of Nakita and the brilliant green of Barnabas. Finding them, I wiped all the threads that were connecting them to Ron's amulet.

Feeling it, Ron swore, dropping back as Barnabas and Nakita both came to life.

A surge of excitement washed through me, and I wavered on my feet with the effort of trying to divide my attention between the now and the next. The minute I quit wiping Ron's amulet's threads, they would be frozen again.

"Leave her alone, Ron!" Barnabas shouted as he caught me, and I felt an odd sensation tingle through my aura. Nakita stood between us, and I wanted to cry. I had freed them! I wasn't so helpless after all, even if Barnabas was keeping me from falling down.

"It's not me," Ron said darkly. "She's just not good at what she's trying to do."

Barnabas's grip on me tightened, and I slowly found my balance. "'S okay," I said softly as dividing my thoughts got easier. I had practiced wiping threads before, but I hadn't done it in a while. Even so, that time I had been destroying the threads my amulet was making, not another's. This was . . . hard, and I couldn't concentrate on everything.

Nakita slowly eased out of her instinctive crouch, knowing Ron wasn't bent on hurting us. He just wanted to know what we were doing. I wasn't going to tell him, and he looked unhappy as I slowly stood under my own power. All we'd have to do was leave, and he'd get nothing.

"What do you want?" I said, though it was obvious. *And who was that with you in the desert? Finding enough time to teach* him, *are you?*

Ron spread his hands wide as he tried to look reasonable. "To know what you're doing," he said. "It's not a scything, or I would have flashed forward by now."

Nakita shifted to put her slight form between me and Ron. "So you can just go, yes?" she said, but he ignored her, looking at Barnabas instead.

"Killing those you once pledged to me to save," Ron said caustically, and I realized that the two hadn't spoken since I'd become the dark timekeeper and Barnabas had left him. "I gave you your amulet. You were my best, Barnabas, but I wouldn't take you back now if you abased yourself on a rock for a thousand years. Consorting with the same dark reaper you fought against? Look at her, with her black nails and shiny purse. She's no warrior. You've yoked yourself to the inept and foolish. You have truly fallen, angel."

"You didn't give me my amulet," Barnabas said tightly. "Your predecessor's predecessor did," he said, releasing his amulet to let the purity of the neutral green shine forth. Nakita and I exchanged a wondering glance. Just how long had Barnabas been at this? "I still believe in choice," he went on stoically. "Times changed. You didn't. I owe you nothing. You lied to me," Barnabas finished bitterly.

"You failed me," Ron said, as if it didn't matter. "I told you to keep your mouth shut. If you had, it would have gone perfectly and light reapers would be in control by now."

"I trusted you to do what is right," Barnabas said softly. "Now I trust Madison."

Ron huffed. "So easily swayed into killing the innocent," the light timekeeper mocked, trying not to look as if he were edging back.

"I'm not," Barnabas said, and Nakita pushed past him.

"And the mark isn't innocent," she said hotly, a flush to her cheeks. "He's deliberately going to allow people to die by his actions, then go on to do it again!"

Alarmed, I shot a look at her. "Shut up!" I exclaimed. She was giving everything away!

But the damage had been done, and Ron's eyes lit up. "It *is* a reap," he said. "But I've not flashed forward."

Nakita struck a dramatic pose. "The seraphs see farther than you."

"Will you shut your mouth!" Barnabas shouted.

"And no worries, Chronos," Nakita boasted, undaunted. "I will kill him before you can set a guardian angel to protect him to his dying days. You won't sully the seraphs' perfect vision this time!"

Great. Just great. This wasn't going well, and I looked into the frozen cornfields as I stood in the middle of an empty road, the sky holding an unmoving sun. "Ron, will you just back off?" I said, knowing he wouldn't. "Whether you believe it or not, I'm trying to save someone."

Barnabas made a strangled noise, and I turned to him. "What, like he hasn't already figured out it's a reap?" I said sourly. "Nakita kind of sank that boat."

Nakita winced with a wash of chagrin, only now realizing what she'd done.

"You," Ron said, pointing a finger at me, "are a murderer for allowing a blood-seeking, avenging angel to scythe the innocent. I tried to save you from it, but you threw your own chance to make a difference in the dirt!"

My eyes narrowed, and I stepped forward until Barnabas's touch stopped me. "Well, maybe if you hadn't lied to me, I might see things differently!" I exclaimed, shaking off Barnabas. Yeah, I was working for the dark reapers, but I was trying to change things, make what the seraphs wanted mesh with what I believed. Ron, though, would never understand.

"I don't care if you believe me or not," I said. "I'm trying to save someone's life. Why don't you just go away?"

Smiling, he slid his gaze to Nakita. She was there to kill Shoe if I failed, and a calculating gleam came into his eye. No matter what, he would always see me in a bad light—chained by what he had believed because it was all he had known.

"You're trying to save someone," he echoed, mocking me. "With a traitorous light reaper who's gone grim and a dark reaper beside you in case you fail."

"I am not a traitor to what I believe!" Barnabas said, and I lifted my chin high.

"We'll find him first," I stated.

Ron chuckled, starting to fall back with a slow toe-heel, toe-heel motion. "We'll see," he said knowingly. "You don't know who you're looking for. You've not flashed forward, either. I can tell. You're far too confident. The seraphs giving you information? Good luck with that. They are so farsighted that they can't see what's under their stuck-up noses. You don't have a clue what you're doing."

"Yeah?" I shot back at him, ticked. "Whose fault is that?"

A huge smile came over his face. "Mine," he said, and still looking at me, he vanished.

The world jumped into motion with a whoosh of sound, and I started, shocked by the sudden burst of new light and noise. My focus blurred as I found myself trying to wipe threads from an amulet that was no longer there. I'd seen him go this time, folding in on himself to vanish in a bright, soundless pop. I'd never be able to do that.

"God help you, Nakita," Barnabas said as he strode out to the middle of the road. "Why didn't you just draw him a picture of who we're trying to save?"

Nakita spun on her heel. "You're still laboring under the assumption that I'm trying to save Shoe," she said, pointing her purse at him as if it were a weapon. "If I so much as see a black wing, light reaper, or guardian angel other than Grace, I will kill him. I will not have that cretin of a timekeeper put a guardian angel on such as Shoe!"

"Ron is not a cretin!" Barnabas shouted, still feeling a smidgen of loyalty, apparently.

"Yes, he is!"

I sighed, sitting down in the middle of the warm road with my back to them, waiting for them to finish yelling at each other. At least Ron had left thinking we didn't know who was marked.

"You are not going to kill Shoe!" Barnabas said. "I won't let you!"

"Careful, Barnabas," she mocked. "Your grim is showing."

That was low, and I turned to see her with a hand on a hip, standing inches from him. He was scowling, feeling the shame of the derogatory term. Barnabas wasn't grim. Sure, he had left Ron, but he wasn't a vigilante who existed only for the thrill of killing someone.

"I won't allow a guardian angel to be gifted to Shoe," she

said, pointing vaguely in the direction of the unseen town. "From the moment he chooses to kill, he will cause only pain to the world. There is no grace in a life lived like that!"

"Funny, isn't that what you do? Kill people?" he shot back at her, and she made a muffled scream of frustration.

"Shut your singing hole," she hissed at Barnabas. "All this arguing is going to get Madison in trouble. The seraphs are watching."

"Then you shut up," he huffed, but I felt a new worry mix with the old. I'd forgotten that. The seraphs were watching, and if I couldn't get a light and a dark reaper to work together, then this would never work.

"Barnabas," I interrupted, not looking up from my view of the cornfield. "Does Ron's knowing what we're doing make this impossible, or just harder?"

Finally they stopped arguing. Barnabas's steps were silent in his faded sneakers as he came to stand in front of me. His wings were gone, and he looked haunted. Clearly Ron had shaken him. "Until Ron can identify who the mark is, I think nothing has changed," Barnabas said, and Nakita snorted. "We'll need to be more circumspect to keep him from following us. One of us needs to stay with you and hide your amulet's resonance." His gaze went behind me to Nakita. "It'd be easier if you'd simply agree not to kill Shoe."

"I have not killed him!" she protested, stalking forward. "But I will before I let Chronos or one of his reapers put an angel on him to protect him from his fate. An angel is forever, and with heaven's mindless protection, he could do untold damage."

I wondered how many of history's recent dictators had been the result of Ron's sending a light reaper to uphold a soul's right to choice. Getting to my feet, I sighed. "This is really weird," I said as I brushed my black tights off. "I like both of you, and I don't know why."

Nakita blinked, her attention diverted from Barnabas. "Because you're the dark timekeeper," she said, as if it were obvious.

Sighing, I looked up and down the road, wanting to be somewhere else. Anywhere else. "What do you think he's going to do?" I asked Barnabas. "Ron, I mean. You know him best."

Barnabas looked to the spot of pavement where Ron had last stood. "Probably search the local time lines until he finds out where we've been, then try to identify the people we've come in contact with. But he won't be able to actually act until he flashes forward and sees the future. That's when he would send a reaper out. Sometimes the dark timekeeper flashes first, sometimes the light. It's the person who flashes last who has the clearer picture of the mark, so it evens things out, I suppose."

I nodded, thinking it made sense. The closer in time the flash was from the turning point happening, the clearer the timekeeper's perceptions would be. Grimacing, I glanced at my watch. It was getting late, and it was going to take a while to get home, even by wing. "I have to get back to school," I said, worried. "Check in with my dad. Get my assignments from Josh."

"I'll stay here," Barnabas said immediately, and Nakita predictably bristled.

"Why you?" she asked belligerently, standing with her feet spread wide.

I met Barnabas's eyes, telling him without saying a word that I'd handle this. She was mad enough at him already. "Because Barnabas won't kill Shoe if Ron sends someone to watch us." Nakita started to protest, and I got angry. "Look," I said, letting some of my frustration show. "There are no black wings in sight. I haven't flashed forward yet, and neither has Ron. Barnabas, can you reach my thoughts over that great a distance?"

"Not when you're shielded," he said glumly.

"Not a problem," I said, running a hand over the back of my head to smooth my hair. "I don't need to be shielded when I'm at home. Ron knows where I live, and if he sees me there, then he might give up on watching me at all. Nakita can fly me home and back again when my dad goes to sleep. You can let us know if something shifts in the meantime."

It was a good plan, as far as I could tell, but Barnabas looked as excited about it as Nakita did. "I'll call you if something changes," he agreed, gaze downcast, and I realized it bothered him that his resonance had officially shifted down the spectrum. He could no longer be counted among the light reapers, no matter what he believed. His contact with me had stained him as much as it had damaged Nakita.

"Okay," I said meekly, not liking to see him depressed. He had been a light reaper for a long time. He wasn't ever going to fit in with the dark reapers, even if his amulet shifted as black as mine. He was going to be alone and apart for the rest of his life.

I edged toward Nakita, never having flown with her before but figuring that if Barnabas could do it, she could, too. For a moment it looked as if she were going to protest, but upon seeing how unhappy Barnabas was, she simply arched her wings to make the tips touch high above her head. I stared up at them, thinking they were beautiful, even if they didn't go with her brightly colored clothes and sandals. I eyed Barnabas, feeling funny leaving him when he was like this.

"Are you able to fly with another person?" I asked her, and Nakita flicked her gaze to Barnabas and back to me.

"I'll let you know in a moment," she said, making me glad I was already dead.

Seeing us getting ready to leave, Barnabas mustered a smile. "Go," he said. "I'll get myself in a distant place where I can watch Shoe without giving away who I'm watching. I'd think we have at least until midnight for Ron to pick out Shoe's resonance from the fabric of time."

By his uneasy stance, I didn't know if I should believe him. Sighing, I dropped back to stand with Nakita. Her arm hesitantly wrapped around my waist, and I stumbled as her wings opened, making us lift an inch and then drop. My heart pounded, and she shifted her weight.

"I'm sorry you're different now," she said to Barnabas. Her words were soft, but I knew he heard her as his shaggy mop of hair shifted. "She changes people," she said, as if I weren't standing right there. "Maybe that's her purpose."

"Maybe," Barnabas said; then he ducked as Nakita pushed down with her wings.

I gasped as the corn around us flattened and we were suddenly airborne. The sudden air-pressure shift made me wince—not to mention Nakita's wobbly ascent—and I looked down as Barnabas gazed up. He was standing in the middle of the deserted road, the impressions of Nakita's wings making what looked almost like part of a crop circle around him. My stomach lurched, and I gripped Nakita's arm holding me to her. She wasn't as good as Barnabas in carrying my weight, but she could do it, and I relaxed, hearing her sigh in relief.

As she winged us back to Three Rivers, my mind kept swirling over the fact that Nakita had felt sorrow for Barnabas when she had once felt only disdain. I had changed her, too.

Devoting your life to the person who had accidentally put black wings inside of you to eat your memories and teach you the meaning of death could not be an easy thing to do.

Five

The spaghetti sauce smelled spicy, just the way I liked it. Or *had* liked it. I sent my fork twirling, winding up a wad I was going to pass to Josh as soon as my dad looked away. Being dead sucked dishwater. I'd never realized how much I had enjoyed food until I couldn't. Sitting across from me in my dad's kitchen, Nakita pushed her food around as well. Josh wasn't helping her eat her spaghetti, and my dad was starting to look worried at her full plate.

"Too much oregano?" he asked, pushing his glasses to the bridge of his nose.

"It's great, Mr. A," Josh said cheerfully around his full mouth.

My dad's eyes were on me, though, and I smiled, forcing myself to put a forkful in my mouth and chew. It just wasn't the same. The solid illusion of my body took what it needed from my amulet. I didn't need outside energy to exist, and the desire to eat just wasn't there. I could do it, but it was like chewing on rice cakes.

"Top-notch, Dad," I said, but it was clear by his suspicious *mmmm* that he didn't believe me. "I had a snack when I got home from school," I said, mentally adding, *Last year, when I was a junior*, to sort of try to keep it from being a lie.

"Well, don't tomorrow, okay?" he said, wiping his fingers on a napkin before taking a sip of his water. "I'm tired of making food that sits on your plate."

My dad stood and went to open the window over the sink. Early cricket song and the hush of a passing car on our quiet residential street slipped in with the golden haze of a low sun. I quickly exchanged forks with Josh, and Nakita frowned. She was going to have to get rid of her food another way. Josh was eager enough, but he wasn't that big a guy.

Nakita and I had gotten back about three thirty to find Josh on my front steps, looking good as he sat with a stack of new textbooks. I owed him big. Bigger than dinner at my house. I had checked in with my dad from the house phone and then we'd sat around in the backyard, watching Josh eat chips as I'd told him the story. Josh had listened to it all, clearly disappointed that he hadn't been there.

It was about seven, and I was getting anxious about Shoe. Ron must have found something out by now, but Barnabas hadn't said a word, meaning the status quo hadn't changed. Sighing, I wound up another wad of spaghetti and passed it over to Josh, who cheerfully took it, head bobbing and mouth still chewing the last forkful. My dad's shoes scraped on the faded linoleum when he turned back around, and I breathed in the scent of oil and ink that clung to him from work as he came back to the table. His thoughts were clearly not on dinner. They were probably on me.

My dad was the classic lab rat, kind of tall, thin, geeky maybe when he had been younger, more comfortable in a lab coat than a tie or trendy shirt. Apart from the gray starting to show in his hair and the faint smile wrinkles around his eyes, he looked the same as he had when he and my mom had separated almost ten years ago.

Mom had moved to Florida with me in tow. She was a variable funds procurement expert, which basically meant she was a hired gun for reputable charities. Her specialty was seducing money from old women—something she was really good at but that was a constant source of strife between us when I couldn't stomach putting on my white gloves and serving as a prop in her spiel. My dad had stayed here.

The rumble of thunder was faint but growing stronger, and the haze of sun coming in the window dimmed as the clouds overtook it. An early dusk was starting to take hold. I skated another wad of spaghetti around on my plate, cringing when I met Nakita's eyes. She had an entire plateful. I made a nod toward Josh for her to give him at least a forkful, and her lips pressed as she thought it over.

My dad sat down and leaned back, assessing me as he chewed. "You two ladies don't look too skinny," he said, his brown eyes still holding a layer of hurt.

"What?" I stammered, looking down at myself.

"Must be a high school–girl thing," he added, smiling at Nakita. "Tell you what. How about you help me make dinner tomorrow night, Madison? Whatever you want."

Josh snorted, hunched over his plate, and I winced, remembering making dinner with my dad when I'd been five. Having a preschooler cook peas did not make her any more eager to eat them, but my parents choking down the barbecue-sauce-laced veggies had been hilarious to my five-year-old self. The evening had ended in giggles and laughter. Maybe we should have had barbecue peas more often. "Okay," I said, eyes lowered as I remembered.

Again my dad made that *mmmm* sound, as if looking into the future. Or maybe the past. A melancholy sadness had taken me, and I forced down a bite of pasta, trying to enjoy the tang of tomatoes and the musky sweetness of the oregano.

I'd been shipped up here almost six months ago, right at the tail end of my junior grade. I'd missed my prom and everything. What had been the straw that broke my mom's camel's back was still a mystery. It could have been the cops bringing me in for breaking curfew when she thought I'd been upstairs on the internet. Or my going to that beach party when I said I wasn't, or that twilight cruise with the guys and swimming around the far buoy—which was totally not my fault. I'd called to say where I was. My mom had nearly popped her pearls that time.

But for whatever reason Mom had decided to ship me back north, I was glad for it, and I smiled as I looked at the ugly wallpaper with yellow roses on it that I vaguely remembered from my childhood. I had thought it was going to be a transfer from one unreasonable jailer to another, but getting to know my dad again had been a pleasant surprise, especially when he actually listened to me when I told him why I had to have one pair of sandals over another. My mom didn't get my sense of style at all. My dad didn't, either, but at least he tried.

In all seriousness, I was trying to be good. I hadn't snuck out of the house in almost a week, apart from the time I had to keep black wings off of Josh. I called when I was going to be late, and I was always here for dinner unless I was pretending to eat at Josh's house. It would get harder, though, if I were fighting off dark timekeepers and trying to save souls.

"All of you are very quiet," he said out of nowhere, and I jerked my head up. "School okay today?"

Crap, he wants to talk about school?

"I'm taking home economics," Nakita offered hesitantly, seeing me almost panicking.

A faint grimace crossed my dad's face, but he relaxed, putting an elbow on the table. "I hated that class. Do they have you making book bags this year?"

Nakita wedged the wad of pasta off her fork and started to wind up another spool. "Why would a book need a bag?"

"Uh, Nakita and I are taking photography together," I broke in, trying to distract him from her puzzled expression. For all my dad knew, Nakita was from Nova Scotia and spoke French as her first language. That the school thought she was living at my house was a bit of angel intervention. No one had bothered to check whether she was. Actually, I didn't know where she went when she left.

Josh ate a bite of bread. "We've got physics together," he said around his food. "Yay."

I smiled at his lackluster exclamation. "It was great to get back and see everyone," I said as I wound up another fork of pasta.

My dad smiled knowingly. "This year will be better. Just you watch," he predicted as he pulled a chunk of bread from the loaf and dipped it in the olive oil and vinegar. "And then college."

"Can I get through physics first?" I asked with a moan. "At least I've got photography this year. That will be fun."

My dad's head bobbed. "That reminds me," he said, glancing over my shoulder at the corkboard by the phone on the wall. "I got a call from your photography teacher with a list of class supplies. Why on earth didn't she just give it to you when you were at school?"

"Ms. Cartwright?" I asked, feeling a flush of worry, and he nodded. "Um, maybe she didn't know at the time," I offered, trying not to lie. *Great,* I thought as I glanced at Josh, who shrugged.

"Do you need to run out to the mall tonight?" my dad asked, his gaze touching on Nakita's black fingernails.

"I can take you," Josh volunteered, clearly seeing a way to get back into the scythe prevention, but my first impulse to say yes died. It would be a great way to slip off my dad's radar for a couple of hours, but I couldn't leave until he thought I was in bed.

"Uh, no," I stammered, and Josh stifled his disappointment. "I've probably got most of it upstairs." I hadn't seen the list, but I had all my stuff from last year.

"I need a camera," Nakita said suddenly, her voice worried.

"I've got one you can borrow," I said quickly. "Don't worry about it, Nakita."

She wiped her lips with a napkin. "I've never used one before. I don't want to break it."

Nakita seemed genuinely concerned, and my dad laughed. "If it's the one I'm thinking of, you can't." He put an elbow on the table and leaned in. "Madison used to be really rough on her cameras, but you can't blame her. She's been taking pictures since she was four. How long have you been behind the lens?"

Nakita blinked, surprised as she always was when my dad

tried to include her in the conversation. My dad liked her, thought the quiet studiousness she showed him would settle me down. But I could probably bring home a biker chick and he'd ask her to stay for dinner, seeing it as proof that I wasn't moping around upstairs by myself, or avoiding people, like I had been when I first moved up here. That I had *two* friends over for dinner had probably made his week.

"Not long," she said, as in *never*, then added, "I'm not creative. I'm there because Madison thinks it will help me fit in."

"At a new school," I blurted.

"I'll never be able to take pictures like Madison," Nakita said.

"Yeah," Josh exclaimed as he wiped the last of his sauce up with a scrap of bread. "Madison takes great pictures."

"Ah!" my dad exclaimed, making me jump. "Everyone has creativity. You just need to stretch your muscles. Madison's been at it a long time," he said, his focus going distant in memory. "She probably doesn't remember it, but I used to take her with me when I'd go out to remote sites for samples. Her mother gave her a camera to keep her busy."

"I remember," I said, wondering if Dad would notice if I switched plates with Josh. I'd tried to throw out the photo albums of corners and clouds almost three years ago, but my mom had rescued them from the trash and hidden them somewhere. "I've got my old camera upstairs." And seeing a way to get out of there, I stood, taking my almost-full plate in hand.

"You're finished?" my dad exclaimed, looking up at me with a lost expression when Nakita followed my lead. Josh blinked up at us, then snatched a last piece of bread as he stood, too.

Again, guilt hit me, even as I dumped the food and turned on the tap to rinse the plate. My dad had been really great since I'd moved back, making me feel wanted and yet giving me the space I needed. Dying and not being able to tell anyone had seemed to put a bigger wall between us than when we had been separated by a thousand miles.

But I couldn't dismiss the feeling that he recalled the night I had died. It wasn't that he ever said anything, but there was a hesitation now where there hadn't been one before. Barnabas had fixed it so my dad didn't remember, but I think he did—on some level. And I didn't want to be alone with him, afraid he was going to bring it up.

Nakita was silent as she threw her food away. Beside her, Josh rinsed his plate off. "I'd better get home," Josh said, sounding disappointed. I'd love it if he could have come with me back to Fort Banks, but Nakita could carry only one. "I've got time to help with the dishes, though," he added.

"Nakita and I have them okay," I offered quickly. *I sort of owe you*, I thought, but I didn't say it. "You probably want to get home before it rains."

"I can drive in the rain," Josh said with a grin.

My dad pushed back and joined us at the sink. "Thanks for coming over, Josh," he said brightly. "I like having a noisy house and cooking for more than one."

"Dad . . ." I complained. "I'm just not hungry."

He didn't say anything, eyebrows high. Josh wiped his hands on his jeans, rocking back from the sink as he looked at me, clearly wanting to say something. "I have to get my stuff," he finally said, then ducked out of the kitchen to leave an uncomfortable silence.

Nakita brought the plate of bread to the sink, hesitating only a moment before reaching for the bag to put it in. "Can we do the dishes later?" I asked my dad. "I want to . . ." *I want to what?* I thought in panic. I couldn't admit I wanted to talk to Josh! My dad might think he was my boyfriend or something. I mean, he sort of was, but it wasn't like we'd even kissed or anything. Yet.

"Go, go, go," he said, making a shooing motion. "I'll clean up. You go talk to Josh."

Nakita was scowling. She didn't like Josh much. I, though, was delighted, and I spun around, wiping my hands on the drying towel. "Thanks, Dad!"

"I have to call Officer Levy back anyway," he said, looking at the clock on the stove.

Officer Levy? Oh, crap.

I rocked to a stop. Nakita and I exchanged looks, mine worried, hers peeved, probably at Barnabas for stopping her from scything the woman. My dad, though, didn't look concerned as he pulled himself up to his full height.

"Dad, I can explain," I started. *How am I going to explain?* I thought, mentally cursing Barnabas. This was the second time he had changed people's memories, only to have them return enough to complicate my life. It probably came from his previous habit of save-the-human-then-split. He never had to deal with people remembering the lies he told them to believe.

But my dad didn't appear to be upset as he rinsed out his glass. "She called me at work. Something about making sure you had a permit to park in the school lot," he said, sounding amused as he worked the taps. "I told her you didn't have a car, and she got confused. But in any case, she wanted to talk to me about a fund-raiser."

"Oh," I said, relaxing. Behind him, Nakita's eyes were a steady blue. If they had gone silver, she would have been doing damage control. Whatever Barnabas had done was apparently holding. "Well, I guess we don't have to worry about a car, huh?" I said sourly, and he sighed. I'd been moaning about my car being down in Florida since I got here, and his answer was always the same: "Not yet."

But this time, instead of giving his pat answer, he turned to me with worried eyes and asked, "Madison, is everything okay?"

I could hear Josh thumping down the stairs, and I nodded, shoving the drying towel over the rack when I realized I was winding it about my fingers. "Trust me, Dad," I said, with what

I hoped was the right amount of annoyance and sincerity as I walked backward to the hallway, snagging Nakita on the way. "I like it here. I'm not going to screw it up. I have friends now and everything. Even if I don't have a car."

His attention flicked to Nakita, and, smiling, he said, "Just promise you'll tell me if you need to talk. I can't help if I don't know what's broken."

It was too close to what I really wanted—to come clean and ask his advice. But what I did was yank the class supply list from the fridge and mutter, "It's just normal teen stuff."

"'Normal' and 'teen' don't go together," he said, and I edged to the archway to the hall. "Call your mom tonight, okay?" he added when Nakita slipped out before me. "She called this afternoon, wanting to talk to you. Right during school hours. I told her you can't have a phone on in school and to calm down, but you know your mom."

His voice held an old frustration, and I halted in the archway, watching him relive the past. I, though, was a little more concerned with the present. My mother was a thousand miles away, and her trouble radar was still working. "I'll call her. And thanks for letting Nakita spend the night."

"I don't know how I let you talk me into stuff like this," he grumped as he turned to the sink and rolled up his sleeves. "I was never allowed to have anyone sleep over, much less on a school night."

Smiling, I came back in, going up on tiptoe to give him a

kiss on the cheek. It was stubbly, and he smelled like . . . Dad. "Because I'm your favorite," I said, bringing back a family joke that hadn't been said in ten years.

My dad smiled, wiping away all my uneasy feelings. "My one and only," he said, giving me an awkward hug as he tried not to get soap suds on me. "Lights out at ten. I mean it!"

We were cool, and, walking with a lighter step, I went into the hallway to find Josh standing with Nakita, his book bag over his shoulder. Seeing me, he let it slide to the floor. From the kitchen, the rush of water filling the sink drifted out.

Josh glanced at the kitchen as I came forward. "See you tomorrow?" he said, and I nodded. It would probably be over one way or another by sunup.

"Thanks for everything," I said, looking at his book bag, then winced. "Josh, I'm sorry. I know you wanted to come with us."

His eyes were on the ceiling. "Next time, maybe," he said, making me feel worse.

Nakita crossed her arms over her chest, shifting her weight to one foot. Josh's gaze came back to her, and he frowned. "Do you mind if I talk to Madison alone?" he asked.

She exhaled, eyes rolling. In a huff, she spun on a heel and stomped upstairs. I swear, some of this fitting-in stuff she picked up fast.

I was still smiling when I brought my attention back to Josh. But seeing his eyes light up when I looked at him, I felt a spark of nervousness fill me. *He wants to be alone with me?*

"Got all your assignments?" he asked, looking at the note in my grip.

"Yes, thanks to you," I said, shoving the note in a pocket. "I really wanted you to come. Nakita can't carry more than one person."

His eyes went to the open archway to the kitchen. "It's okay," he said, dropping a step back to the door. "Just don't make me into the librarian guy who looks things up for you and always misses out." He smiled. "Dinner was good."

"I'll take your word on that."

Josh took his truck keys from his pocket and reached for the door behind him. "Well, I'll see you tomorrow," he said, slinging his book bag over his shoulder.

Disappointment seeped into me, but what had I expected? It wasn't like we'd been on a date—except for last year's prom, and that was a disaster. Reaching out, I touched his hand. Josh halted, the door cracked open.

"Thank you," I whispered. "Josh, I mean it."

He looked down at our hands, then at the kitchen where my dad was noisily putting dishes in the dishwasher. "Will your dad freak if I kiss you good-bye?" he asked.

I blinked, my heart giving a thump before I stopped it. "Probably," I said, feeling breathless. I'd kissed boys before—my mom didn't ground me because I was a saint—but I'd been flaking out lately about being dead and had been holding myself apart. That he might want to kiss me thrilled me down to my toes.

Josh took my hand more firmly. From the kitchen came a clatter of pans in the sink. I held my breath, feeling the memory of my heart pound all the harder. "Don't forget about me?" he whispered, his head beside mine, not kissing me, but really close.

The scent of spaghetti, bread, and shampoo filled me with a feeling of security. "Never," I said, meaning it. Tilting my head, I closed my eyes. Our lips touched, like I hoped they would. Warm against mine, his were hardly there before he dropped back. A quiver rose and fell through me, and my eyes opened, finding his. He was smiling softly. It had happened too fast, and he ducked his head when the silverware clinked. I felt flushed, warm. Excited and calm all at the same time.

"I should go," he said, hoisting his bag to his shoulder again.

"Yeah," I said, wondering how something so simple made the world look so different.

"See you tomorrow, Madison," he added, glancing at the kitchen.

"Bye." I really didn't want him to go.

Josh reached out, taking my hand and then letting it slip from his as he walked through the door and shut it behind him.

I let go of a breath I'd taken who knew how long ago, my attention flicking to the kitchen when my dad shouted through the open window, "Bye, Josh. Take it easy going home."

"You got it, Mr. A," came back faintly, and I turned to the stairway, jerking when I saw Nakita waiting for me at the top. Josh hadn't given any indication that she'd been there, but I knew from her bothered expression that she'd seen the entire thing.

"He kissed you," she said before I was even halfway up.

"You want to say that a little louder?" I said sourly. "My dad might not have heard you."

She stepped aside as I came even with her, her posture uneasy. "It made your pulse start," she said, falling into step behind me.

"Yep," I said, smiling. Through the house, I heard Josh's truck rev. My thoughts were still on him as I flopped onto my bed. He really was a nice guy.

Nakita shut the door behind her. "Do you think I should paint my nails?"

The shift of topics pulled my attention from the ceiling, and I propped myself up on an elbow. "You saw my dad look at them?" I asked, and she nodded, her beautiful face holding an almost comical amount of worry. "If you want."

"I want to," she said, looking relieved now. "And my toes."

"I like them the way they are," I said, rolling onto my stomach to reach the bedside table. Pulling it open, I rummaged until I found a bright red that went with her purse, now sitting on my dresser beside our textbooks. Josh had brought them over, too. Man, I really owed him.

"Good?" I asked as I held it up to her.

Nakita took it, her expression empty. "Do you have a paler color?"

I suddenly realized she was trying to look normal—to fit in—and I rolled back to look again. "I've got pink," I said, and Nakita visibly relaxed.

"Thank you."

She was all smiles again. Thinking that anyone else would get labeled with bipolar disorder, I shoved the drawer shut and dug the photography class–supplies list out of my pocket, going over the crumpled paper and mentally comparing it to what I had in my closet. "Most of this I've got," I said, rolling over and finding my feet. "Do you want my red camera or the black one?"

"Black. No, red," she said immediately, and then followed it with, "Which one would you pick?"

I opened my closet. Hands on my hips, I looked for the box I'd stashed them in. Josh said I took great pictures. My dad had said the same thing, but hearing it come from Josh so casually left me feeling warm—when warmth was something I hadn't felt in months.

"There it is," I said softly, leaning in past my skirts, tops, and jeans to reach the box in the back. It was from my mother's grocery store, and I felt a twinge of homesickness as I set it on my desk. *Call Mom. Don't forget.*

The unmistakable scent of electronics sifted out when I opened it up, tickling memories. "The red one is newer, but the black one has more versatility," I said, and when she blinked vacantly at me, I handed her the black one. "This one takes better pictures. It doesn't focus automatically, and you can choose what you focus on. Sometimes shooting something fuzzy makes it easier to see what you're trying to show."

Okay, it didn't make much sense, but she took the old camera, carefully unzipping her purse and setting it inside. I swore I saw her smile as the up-to-now-useless bag suddenly had a purpose. It was the only thing in there.

"You can keep the nail polish, too," I said, thinking that a purse should really have more than one thing in it.

"Thank you," she said seriously as she set the bag beside her books and kicked off her sandals like a normal person. Normal, yes, but the wedges landed neatly under my wide window as if having been placed there. "I'll never be as good as you," she said wistfully.

I glanced at her perfect feet, then looked away. Jeez, no wonder the guys fell over themselves to talk to her. Even her feet were beautiful. "Being as 'good' as someone else isn't the goal," I said, dropping back on the bed to stare at my ceiling. I'd call my mom later. "Finding a way to show how something makes you feel is. There's no wrong way to take a picture. If it makes you feel something, then you've done it right."

The bed moved as she sat down on the end, and I shifted my weight. "Do you think your dad will like them?" she asked. "My pictures, I mean."

Nakita was so confident of herself when she was on a scythe, it was odd to see her so unsure. "I know he will." A smile curved up the corners of my mouth as I imagined her showing them to him. My dad loved my photography. He had an entire wall in the formal dining room devoted to my stuff, with lights shining on his favorites and everything. He was the one who told me about capturing how something makes you feel, and I think he tried to figure out what was going on in my head by what was coming out of my printer.

The biting smell of polish was strong. This waiting-around stuff was aggravating, but we couldn't leave until my dad was in bed. My gaze drifted, finding the picture of Wendy and my ex-boyfriend, Ted, on my mirror. They looked happy together on the beach at sunset. I rolled over so I could see my old friends upright. I'd let go of the idea of Ted in my life almost as soon as I'd moved up here. Guys were like puppies sometimes—loyal but easily distracted—and I had known that as soon as I was gone, he'd find someone else to follow around. That it had been my best friend, Wendy, wasn't a surprise. Squinting, I wondered if I could see a haze of blue around Wendy, mixing with a shadow of yellow about Ted. Their auras? My thoughts flitted back to Josh and that first kiss. And I smiled.

"Do you think Barnabas is doing okay?" I asked Nakita.

"I don't know. I can't reach him," she said, sounding almost catty.

Jeez, what is with her tonight? I turned, seeing her bent at a sharp angle to put her face near her toes. Her hair draped to one side, framing her strong cheekbones and accentuating her perfect complexion. Her amulet gently swayed as she covered her black nails in pink, hiding what she was. Frankly, she looked like a model. Me, I was too flat chested, and since I was now dead, I was stuck waiting for the boob fairy for the rest of my existence. *Isn't that nice . . . ?*

Nakita knew I couldn't contact Barnabas, but that didn't mean I'd have to waste the next couple of hours. My body was somewhere between the now and the next, according to the seraph who had witnessed me taking on the role of the dark timekeeper. If I could find it, then I could go back to really living and give up being the boss of a system I didn't agree with. I could forget all about timekeepers, amulets, reapers, and black wings. I could be myself again. Even if it meant forgetting all of this.

Glancing at Nakita, I wondered if that was something I still wanted to do.

Of course it is, I told myself, then stared up at the ceiling, wondering how one found the space between the now and the next.

Silence filled my soul, and I closed my eyes. I didn't know

where to even look. But wherever it was, I probably had to find it using my head, not my eyes. Taking three slow breaths, I held the last one, letting it out slowly until my lungs were empty. It was the first step in Barnabas's "center yourself" exercise.

"What are you doing?" Nakita asked, startling me even though her voice had been soft.

I took a breath. "Besides waiting for my dad to go to sleep? Seeing if I can find the now and the next." It was either that or call my mom.

I heard her shift position and start on the other foot. "Good luck with that."

My eyebrows rose. The modern phrase had sounded odd coming from her. She was mad. "You're fitting in great, Nakita," I said as I opened my eyes and sat cross-legged on my bed. "You sounded almost like a real teenager there."

"You don't want to be a timekeeper," she accused, blue eyes flashing, then amended it, saying sullenly, "You don't want to be the *dark* timekeeper. I think if you had the chance, you'd put a guardian angel on Shoe."

Is that what's bothering her? "I am not going to put a guardian angel on Shoe," I said. "A guardian angel won't accomplish anything." I snatched up the red nail polish and rubbed the bottle between my palms to mix it without putting air into it.

Nakita watched me mix the polish, and I could almost see her file the information away. Eyes coming up, she pressed her lips together and glared. "You don't believe in fate. Soon as you don't need that amulet to stay alive, you'll give it back. And then you'll forget everything. I was there. I heard you tell the seraph."

"Nakita . . ." I coaxed.

"It's okay," she said tightly, and dipped the brush back in the bottle balanced precariously on her bent knee. "I'm a dark reaper. It's my job to kill people. I don't expect you to like me."

This was getting worse and worse. Sighing, I set the bottle on my dresser and carefully opened it. "I do like you," I said, unable to look at her as I put a red stripe on my black nails. "I think you're great. God, Nakita, you can fly!" I looked up. "But I miss sleeping. I like being hungry, and then feeling good after I eat. I feel bad about lying to my dad and changing his memories. And I can't be the boss of a system that I don't believe in. If I can't change things, then I'm going to give it up as soon as I get my body back."

She took a breath to speak. Her eyes fixed on mine, and I couldn't look away. "But you're good at this," she said softly.

I'm good at this? Shocked, I stared at her, and a drop of red hit my comforter. "How so?" I said, dropping the brush into the bottle and scrambling for a tissue. "You've made it clear you think I'm doing the wrong thing. How can I convince the seraphs if I can't even convince you?"

Great. Dad's going to be mad about the comforter, I thought, flustered as I dabbed to get the worst of it, but confusion was pinching her eyes when I looked up.

"I don't know," she said, "but you believe in what you're doing. Timekeepers change for a reason. You're . . . passionate about helping people, even if I don't understand what you're trying to do. The mistakes don't matter. It's what you do when you mess up that does."

I met her lost expression with my own. I understood what she was saying, sort of, but I couldn't have it both ways.

"Besides," Nakita said softly as she turned her attention back to her nails, "I'd miss you if you were gone."

I sat on my bed, two nails painted, the rest still utterly black. I didn't know what to say. My curtains moved in a gust of wind, and a roll of thunder gave her last words more weight. The sun was probably still up, but I couldn't see it behind the dark clouds.

Nakita's sigh mixed with the first drops of rain hitting the roof. I had to say something, but nothing rose through my blissfully empty mind as big plops of rain hit sporadically and the smell of wet shingles drifted in with the breeze. Still searching for something to say that would give her solace and yet make my intentions clear, I moved to close my window.

"Nakita—" I started, gazing out at the early darkness and the flat gray clouds.

But a soft, oh-so-familiar sound scraped across my awareness like a knife. It was the sound of sneakers finding a grip on the roof. And then the soft tinkling of Grace singing, "There once was a boy on a roof, who kept himself far too aloof. Like a snail he did crawl, till he took a big fall. 'Cause really he was a big stupe."

Is Barnabas back? "Barnabas?" I called loudly, leaning out the window.

Nakita looked up from finishing her toenails. A sudden scrabbling from higher up on the roof shocked through me. Reaching for the screen, I lifted it free and set it aside. A yelp of alarm from the roof pulled Nakita to her feet, and with the frightening sound of sliding grit, a white shadow fell past my window. Arms and legs flailing, someone dropped off the roof. A loud thump followed by a groan rose up with the soft roll of thunder.

I turned to Nakita. "I don't think that was Barnabas," I said.

Her face was calm, but her eyes were silver. "I can't tell. Whoever it is, he's shielding his aura." Eager to find out, she handed me her polish. "I'll be right back."

My eyes widened. "Nakita!" I hissed, but she had already sent her hand about her amulet. A shimmer of violet light ran over her, and then her sword appeared in her free hand. "Nakita, wait!" I demanded as I set the polish down, but she was halfway through my window and on the roof.

"Puppy presents on the rug," I whispered as she stood on the edge of the roof and looked at the ground with a hand on her hip. The wind gusted, and the rain pattered down heavier, the branches over my room blocking most of it.

"Who are you?" she said loudly as she looked down; then she dropped out of sight.

"Grace!" I shouted. Okay, it hadn't been Barnabas eavesdropping, but someone was, and Grace had made him fall.

The messenger angel flew in, bringing with her the smell of ozone and rain, darting about in chagrin, if a ball of light could look chagrined.

"Darn it, Madison! I didn't want you to know I was here," she said, sounding disappointed. "I wasn't spying on you. I promise! It was that boy of a rising timekeeper. Paul wasn't being nice, so I made him fall. You weren't supposed to know I was here!"

"Go get Barnabas," I said, my hand on the sill.

"You're not mad?" The glow that was all I could see of her vanished as her wings stopped moving.

"No, but I will be if you don't get Barnabas. He's shielded, and I can't reach him." Actually, I was furious, but I was more concerned about Nakita and whoever had fallen off the roof.

"Be right back," she chimed in relief, and she darted out the window.

Taking a breath, I reached for the window again. A faint huff of surprise came from the yard under my window, followed by a ping. It was more of a feeling than a sound, and a wash of violet colored the underside of the leaves of the oak tree arching over my room.

That did not look good. Pushing the curtains aside, I vaulted onto the warm, damp roof and into the heavy night.

Six

My sneakers slid on the damp grit of the roof, and I sat down fast before I fell off. The branches overhanging the house made the night seem darker, and I carefully scooted to the edge, looking down to find Nakita standing over someone. She had two swords, one in each hand. My lips parted as I recognized the guy, now flat on his back in my yard. I'd seen him in the desert through Ron's eyes. He had an amulet glowing a thick, earthy green. The deep color was echoed in one of the swords Nakita held. His, obviously. Grace had called him Paul.

"Tell me who you are!" Nakita demanded.

Sighing, I dangled my feet and dropped from the eaves, pushing out so I wouldn't snag my tights on the gutters. I hit the ground hard and tugged my skirt down fast. "Nakita! Take it easy!" I said in a loud whisper as the shock of impact shivered up through me.

She turned to me and I added, "I think that's Ron's replacement, Paul."

"Chronos's—" she started, then yelped and jumped back when the guy kicked at her. Sandy, our neighbor's golden retriever, began to bark and jump against the chain-link fence.

The guy scrambled back and up, tugging his clothes straight as he halted well within Nakita's strike range. *Silly mortal.*

"Give me my scythe," he demanded, but Nakita wasn't listening. Neither was Sandy as I told her to shut up. It was raining harder, and everything not under the tree was getting wet.

"You're the rising light timekeeper?" she asked, her face shadowy but her tone clear. "You're hardly old enough."

I winced in sympathy as he clenched his jaw and held out his hand. "Just give me my sword, okay?" His accent was clearly Midwest American, despite his odd clothes—the same billowy shirt and pants I'd seen through Ron's eyes earlier today—which had a martial-arts kind of a look. Leave it to Ron to make him wear funny clothes.

Nakita's chin lifted, and she took a firmer stance. "Why? You were spying on us!"

"Because giving him his sword back is the decent thing to do," I said, wondering how much of Nakita's and my conversation he'd been privy to. Great. I really needed Ron to know Nakita was worried about my betraying her.

Sandy finally shut her yap, and I sidled up alongside Nakita. It was nice to feel in control for once, and I stared right back at him as he ran his attention up and down me once. "Go to hell," he said simply.

Oooh, nice. "New plan. Don't give him his sword," I said, and he retreated into the shadow of the garage and closer to Sandy. The friendly dog began to dig at the fence.

"See? He's rude," Nakita said as she handed me his sword and Paul stiffened.

Paul's sword felt heavy in my grip, kind of tingly, but I knew better than to swing it and tell him I didn't know how to use it. I'd never seen such a pretty stone, though, the green gleam in the hilt matching his amulet perfectly, flecks of gold running through it like a cat's eye.

The guy pulled himself together, clearly not liking my holding it. "I'm not the one killing people for choices they make and deeds they haven't done yet."

"Who, me or her?" Nakita asked.

I shot a look at the open window in my room. "Will you keep it down? My dad's inside," I said, but neither of them was listening. Paul's eyes were still on his sword. Oh, yeah. He wanted it badly. "Where's Ron?" I asked him with a sudden thought, and his face lost its expression. It was dark, but I could still see his face in the faint light from the front porch. The sound of rain grew heavier, and a light mist started to hiss through the leaves, reaching us.

Beside me, Nakita made a small noise of pleasure. "He fears," she said, lifting the point of her sword, and he took another step back toward the fence. "I know fear. I know it better than any reaper ever having taken wing. Chronos doesn't know you're here, and you're afraid." She looked at me, lips quirking. "He reminds me of you. Impulsive."

Gee, thanks, I thought, and Ron's apprentice stiffened.

"I'm nothing like you!" he claimed, then sent his gaze skyward to the sound of wings.

It was Barnabas—Grace, too—and my shoulders eased. The scent of sunflowers suddenly filled the heavy air. A flash of light lit the night, and a crack of thunder rolled over us. Lightning. Yeah, that would finish this off nicely.

"We're good! It's okay!" I said as loudly as I dared, glancing at the bright square of my second-story window. The last thing I needed was another scythe pulled.

Grace made three circles around Nakita and me before darting up into the tree. Paul never looked at her. *Curious . . .*

Nakita tightened her grip on her sword as Barnabas landed in the street. His wings vanished, and looking like himself in a faded tee, jeans, and the gray duster he sometimes wore, he ambled casually across the grass. Sandy's complaints grew loud, her tail brushing the ground like mad and making Paul shift uneasily.

"I know who you are," Paul said to Barnabas, backing up to the fence until the dog jumped at him to make the chain link rattle. "You've gone grim. Filthy turncoat. You're worse even than *them*."

"He's rude!" Grace said. "That's why I made him fall off the roof, to make a big 'oof'!"

I knew Paul's accusation bothered Barnabas, but he seemed unaffected, his pace never faltering as he came even with us . . . and then continued forward. Paul paled. Looking scared, he backed up along the fence, but Barnabas was after the dog, who cheerfully licked him when he murmured a soft greeting to her and pushed his fingers through the chain link.

"Well, well, well," he said lightly as he dried his fingers on his shirt and reached for the unfamiliar sword in my grip. A tingle went through me as he took it, and I shivered. "Look who slipped his leash," he added, studying the green jewel. "You're Ron's replacement, aren't you? Rising timekeeper?"

Paul stubbornly didn't say anything, but it was obvious he was.

"I told you he was," Grace blurted gleefully. "The seraphs saw him leave and sent me to watch him. I was *not* spying on Madison. I knew *Madison* would be okay with Nakita." The angel flew circles around me. "Really, Madison. I wasn't."

"I believe you," I said, and I swear, her wings grew so bright Paul had to notice her. But he didn't, his flicking gaze telling me he thought I was talking to Barnabas.

"He fell off the roof," Nakita said. "He's just as reckless as Madison. It's going to be a very difficult next hundred years until they figure out what they're doing."

Paul frowned. I wasn't so pleased about it, either.

Grace lit up. "Oh!" she exclaimed, finally realizing that Paul had no clue she was there. "He can't see me? Why not?" She darted down to hover before his amulet. "There once was a keeper named Ron, who had the smarts of a prawn. An amulet he made, to his student then gave, but its powers were somewhat a yawn."

Ron gave Paul an inferior amulet? Why am I not surprised? Nakita was laughing, and even Barnabas snickered. "How come you were on my roof?" I asked, eyes fixed on the sparkling jewel as Barnabas turned the blade so it caught the dim light from the front porch.

"That's what I'd like to know," Barnabas said, starting to wield the sword, testing the blade's balance with a series of rapid, intricate swings almost too fast to follow, his duster furling as he moved. I was used to the angel's proficiency, but Paul was staring with openmouthed awe. The sword had been created by Paul's amulet, and until he drew the energy back into the stone, his amulet would be diminished. I'd once taken control of Nakita's amulet by seizing her sword. Paul had a right to be concerned.

"Give me back my sword!" Paul said, and Barnabas looked him up and down as he stopped swinging. The anger in Barnabas's eyes was new, and I didn't like seeing it there.

"Why were you on the dark timekeeper's roof?" Barnabas

demanded, and I realized how much it had bothered him. It bothered me, too, and standing shoulder-to-shoulder with Nakita, we pinned Paul against the fence. Behind him, Sandy whined. It was starting to rain in earnest, and I swear I could smell wet feathers.

Paul was silent, his eyes glinting in the lamplight as his chin rose. I put a hand on my hip, almost ready to let Nakita have her way, when a faint voice from inside shouted, "Madison?"

Crap, it was my dad. Wincing, I looked up at my bright window. It had sounded like he'd called from downstairs, but that could change really fast.

"I'll take care of it," Barnabas said as he handed me Paul's sword. It was warm in my grip, slick from the rain, and again I was struck by how wrong it felt in my grasp. After giving a warning look to Nakita for her to behave, Barnabas jogged to the front door and rang the bell.

"Get back in the shadows," Nakita hissed, and I shifted to stand in the narrow overhang of the garage. This was where I usually got onto the roof when sneaking back in, and I fumbled for the two dog biscuits I had on the garage windowsill, throwing one over the fence to keep Sandy occupied while my dad answered the door. Paul ducked as the dog treat went sailing over his head, the tips of his hair dripping.

"You can't touch me," he said to Nakita, though he, too, looked anxious not to get caught.

"She can outright kill you," I said bluntly, and Grace sighed heavily. "It was a reaper blade that killed me."

Paul's eyes widened, and Nakita smirked. "Didn't know that, did you?" she whispered as my dad opened the front door and Barnabas said hello.

"There once was a man with an ego," Grace sang softly, slowly losing altitude until she landed on the filthy windowsill, "who thought that he was a big hero. Like a dark reaper, he scythed a timekeeper. But it only made him a big zero."

She was talking about Kairos, the timekeeper whose amulet I now had. He'd not only tried to kill me to retain the position, but he'd killed his predecessor to gain the title early.

Paul was properly cowed, so I edged to the front of the garage to peek around the corner. A shaft of light spilled out into the dreary night, illuminating Barnabas and seeming to make him glow around the edges. I knew it was my imagination, but my dad looked pale by comparison.

"Hi, Mr. A," Barnabas said, sounding completely normal. "I know it's late, but I have to take Nakita home."

A pang of guilt struck me, and I winced when my dad's silhouette eclipsed the light and his rumbling voice said, "I thought she was spending the night. Come on in."

"She was," Barnabas said as he wiped his feet and went inside. "But she didn't—"

The door shut, and I never heard the lie.

"Gabriel's broken feathers," Nakita swore, glancing at the

window. "Now I have to go make an appearance. Madison, will you be okay?"

"Sure," I said, hefting Paul's sword. "Just don't take too long." I was going to give Paul his sword back as soon as she got out of sight. If he tried anything after that, Grace would keep him tripping over his own feet.

Unaware of my plans, Nakita gave him a vehement look to behave. Slipping out past the garage roof, she jumped almost straight up, grabbing the overhang of the garage and swinging herself up like a star athlete. It was how I got up there, but I needed the trash can to do it. I was a lot less graceful, too. Getting to her feet, she brushed the grit from her jeans and made the short hop to my window. I heard, more than saw, her slip inside. *Alone at last . . .*

"If he tries anything," Grace said from beside me, "I'm going to sic Sandy on him."

I didn't want to know how she was planning on getting Sandy past the fence. It might involve lightning. Exhaling a breath I'd probably taken two minutes ago, I looked Paul over. "Here," I said, handing him his sword, the point down. "Sorry. Nakita is a little intense."

"Madison!" Grace exclaimed, turning three shades brighter, and I ignored her.

Sure enough, Paul didn't make the smart decision. "I won't let you kill again!" he shouted, and I sprang away as he leaped forward, my back hitting the side of the garage. Something that felt like cold, black feathers slid through me, and I gasped.

"Hey!" I yelled as I realized he had taken a swing at me. "What's your problem, dude?" I exclaimed, ticked as Sandy barked furiously.

Grace was laughing, her voice rising up out of my range of hearing as her glow wildly shifted through the spectrum. I, though, failed to see the humor.

Paul was staring at me, his sword tight in his grip as the rain made trails down his face. "I hit you! I know I hit you!" he said, sounding betrayed. "It went right through you, and you're okay! You really *are* dead!"

"You think?" I said sharply as I tugged at my shirt to see if he'd cut it. Grace was rolling on the grass, a violent red as she laughed. "You want to be dead, too? Just keep it up, you nutcase. What the devil is wrong with you?"

Still he stared, backing up until he hit the fence. Sandy jumped at him, and he took a distracted step forward, wet dog prints probably all over his back. "Ron said you were," he stammered.

"He does occasionally tell the truth." Fortunately Paul's sword was designed to sever souls, not cloth. My shirt was okay. "Do you have any idea how much this cost me?" I asked, relieved I wouldn't have to explain a foot-long tear to my dad. "Just because you run around looking like Luke Skywalker doesn't mean the rest of us want to dress in rags!"

"Paul was a rising timekeeper, who wanted to be like a reaper.

He swung his big sword, like a medieval lord, and it made him look like a creep-er."

"That almost makes sense, Grace," I said, and she found the air again. She glowed softly, and a sifting of dust fell from her as she got rid of the rain dampening her wings.

Paul's eyes darted around when he realized I wasn't as alone as I looked. Unsure, he was silent until our eyes met. "You're not what I thought you'd be."

I shrugged, leaning back against the garage to stay out of the rain and crossing my arms over my chest until I realized it made me look vulnerable, and I put my thumbs in my pockets instead. "Ron told you I was death on roller skates?" I said, still huffy over the sword thing. "Did he tell you that he lied to me about who I was? After I was dead and everything? Did he tell you how he hid my existence from the seraphs so they couldn't give me my body back and I couldn't go back to living? I'm dead, Paul, and it sucks."

Paul dropped his eyes. Grace, too, was silent, probably remembering her part in all of it. Ron had used her as well. A soft roll of thunder came distantly, and the streetlight shone on Paul's wet hair. It looked black now, but when I'd seen him in the desert, it had been brown.

"I didn't want to be the dark timekeeper," I said, and his lips pressed together as if he didn't believe me. "I still don't. I could have gotten my body back right then and given this thing up." I showed him my amulet, wanting him to see how much older mine looked than his. I might not know how to use it, but it was a lot more powerful than the one Ron had made him. "But Ron didn't tell anyone, and by the time the truth came out, Kairos had died and it was too late. Ron told you about him, right?"

"The old timekeeper," Paul said. "You killed him?"

"What part of not being a murderer doesn't he get here?" Grace muttered, and I felt a wash of warmth fill me as she landed on my shoulder.

"No," I said. "Nakita scythed him when she found out that he had lied to her and that I was his replacement. She didn't like that he was trying to go against seraph will by killing me. You know what it's like to have someone trying to kill you?"

I pushed myself forward from the wall of the garage, and he took a half step back. "No."

"It happens to me all the time."

Paul looked at his sword, and Grace took off from my shoulder. For an instant, the sword glowed its entire length. Then it was gone and his hand was empty. A glitter of gold swam in the depths of his amulet, and then that, too, went dark and quiescent. It was just a flat black stone.

"Why did you come here?" I asked, feeling almost depressed. This guy hated me, and he didn't even know me.

Paul looked to the street, then to me. "Ron said you claimed you were trying to save someone. But it's your job to send reapers to end lives early. I wanted to see for myself."

He hadn't believed Ron. More curious.

Grace's wings blurred into existence, and she whispered, "I told you I wasn't spying on you. The seraphs fated him to meet you tonight, and I was sent to make sure you both survived."

Oh, really? That was . . . disturbing. Filing that away, I straightened. "And?" I asked.

Behind him, Sandy quietly sat in the rain, her tail getting muddier as she waved it in the dirt. "Well, you are the dark timekeeper," he said sullenly.

"Being dark does not mean bad," I said hotly. "Light is for human choice, easily seen. Dark is for hidden seraph fate, no choice to glean." I took a slow breath. He could leave now if he wanted to—the fact that he hadn't said a lot. Or maybe it just meant he wanted something. "My name is Madison," I said in case Ron hadn't told him.

He hesitated, then cautiously said, "I'm Paul."

"And I'm Grace. Put a smile on your face. For the whole human race. Get off Madison's case. There's got to be a poem in there somewhere," Grace muttered, rising up and away.

I felt alone. Paul looked silly standing there in the rain, his hair plastered to his forehead and water dripping from his hem. "Do me a favor, Paul," I said. "Tell Ron I want him to back off. I'm trying to save this guy. Ron's butting in is what will trip Nakita into . . . ah, doing her thing," I finished, not wanting to say "killing him." "Whether you think so or not, I believe in choice as much as you do."

Paul laughed bitterly. "Choice? Dark timekeepers don't believe in choice."

"Yes, I know," I moaned. "But there it is, okay? I'm trying to find a way to do my job in a way that doesn't go against all I believe in. Give me a break, will you?" I was getting frustrated, and the more agitated I got, the more confident he became—even soaking wet and standing in the rain.

Water slipping down his neck, he said, "Why not just tell me who the mark is, and we can put a guardian angel on him?"

I thought back to Nakita's words not an hour ago, and felt ill. If I had promised her not to, would I have said yes now? "Is that your answer?" I said, wishing Barnabas would hurry up. "Put a guardian angel on him? Can you *think* any more short-term? Besides, the guy is slime, Paul. He is going to cause a lot of pain and heartache for kicks unless something happens to change his path."

"Then you've flashed forward," he said softly.

"No," I said, not liking to admit that I wasn't capable of doing real timekeeper stuff. "The seraphs told me."

"And you believe them." His expression was ugly, as if the seraphs were the bad guys.

"They have no reason to lie."

Paul, though, had stopped listening. The squeak of my front door opening sparked through me, and I tossed Sandy the last dog bone. "I'm trying to talk to him," I said as Barnabas and Nakita came out arguing. "If I can help this guy change his life, then fate might not dictate that it be ended. That's it. That's all I'm doing. Now, will you get Ron to back off and let me make a real try of it? Soon as a light reaper or black wings show, I'm going to have a hard time keeping Nakita from—"

"Killing him," Paul finished for me, his eyes hard. "Everyone has a right to make a choice, wrong or not."

"I'm not arguing with you," I said as Barnabas and Nakita approached. "But why allow someone to make a bad choice when a little information might engender a better one? It's hard to wake up and see the sun if the blinds are pulled. I'm a blind puller, Paul. Stop trying to yank me from the window."

He thought about that, glancing at the approaching reapers. "Tell me who you're going to scythe," he demanded before they got close enough to hear. "Maybe then I'll believe you."

"I won't betray Nakita," I said softly over the hissing rain. "She's my friend."

"It would be easier if you did."

The sound of Barnabas's steps grew close, and I backed up to make room for him. Nakita had her purse, swinging it as if she wanted to use it like a hammer. I knew I looked flustered, and when Barnabas saw my empty hands—and realized that Paul had his sword back—he sighed. "Madison," he complained.

Clearly we weren't going to get anywhere new, and just wanting Paul to go, I said, "Paul was just leaving," then turned to him. "Right?"

Barnabas muttered, "You'd better call Ron, then. I'm not flying him home."

"I don't need to be flown home," Paul said, and with a sly arching of his eyebrows, he sort of slid sideways and vanished in a shimmering line of black.

"Holy crap!" I exclaimed, dropping back in shock. "I can't do that!" I spun to Barnabas and Nakita. "How come I can't do that?" Jeez, he could have left anytime after he'd gotten his sword back. Why hadn't he?

"You can," Nakita said, quickly recovering.

"You just don't know how," Barnabas added.

Grace made a sharp sound of surprise. "I got it, I got it!" she cried. "My name is Grace, from heavenly space. I'm watching Paul, whose ass has hauled. I gotta make haste." And in that same sort of sliding sideways light, she vanished.

Peeved, I tucked my amulet behind my damp shirt in disgust. "Don't these things come with a manual?" I grumbled. One good thing had come out of this, though: If Grace was watching Paul, she wasn't watching me.

Barnabas shivered, his wings appearing to glow in the streetlight. "We're leaving?" I guessed, and Barnabas nodded, his wings arching to cover me. "What about my dad?"

No one said anything, and I turned to Nakita, seeing her lips pursed. My thoughts went back to them arguing as they left my house. "What about my dad?" I asked again, louder.

Barnabas took my arm and drew me closer. "He's on the couch, watching TV."

He smelled like wet feathers, and I pushed his hand off me. "What did you do to my dad?" I accused, and he flushed.

"Nothing!" he exclaimed. "Come on. I can dry you on the way." I didn't move, and he shot Nakita a look to shut up when she took a breath. "Okay, okay," he added. "I simply gave him a memory that you're in bed already. I'm not leaving you and Nakita here, and I can't leave Shoe for much longer. Your dad will be fine. Can we get through the clouds and above the rain, please?"

From the shadows, a dark-winged Nakita grumbled that she could have done a better job of handling my dad.

Standing there with the rain misting my face, I wondered if Paul was right. I could have given him Shoe's name, and then it would have been over. Except Shoe would spend the rest of his charmed life causing mayhem. And more important, I would have betrayed Nakita's trust.

Hesitating, I looked at Barnabas. The rain dripped from the ends of his flattened hair as he silently waited, a question in his pinched brow. With a sudden flash of clarity, I realized he had intentionally drawn Nakita into the house so I could do just that. He had given me the opportunity to tell Paul who we were after.

And when I smiled at him and shook my head, he seemed to relax. He hadn't wanted me to, but he'd given me the chance.

Somehow, that made me feel good. Like I'd finally done something right.

Nakita looked from me to him and back again, knowing something unsaid had crossed between us, but not what. "Are we going?" she asked slowly.

"Absolutely," I said, and Nakita smiled. I believed in choice, but giving Shoe a guardian angel wasn't choice. It was a cop-out.

Seven

I was glad my body wasn't real as I crouched outside Shoe's window, because my knees would be aching right about now. I straightened, shifting to stand beside the window and get a glimpse of his tidy bed. Beside me, Barnabas watched Shoe, his brown eyes unblinking. Nakita was wandering about the front yard, snapping pictures of leaves, trees, and a crack in the sidewalk, making me nervous even though she had the flash off. At least it wasn't raining here. Small favors.

While airborne, I had dried to a sort of sticky moistness, and I envied Barnabas's ability to somehow dry completely. Nakita, too, was arid in her jeans and sandals, her fingernails now matching her toes in their pearly pinkness. She'd finished painting them just moments before, bored with it all.

"Can't we just go and talk to him?" I whispered when Nakita

ranged close again, taking a picture of what looked like nothing. I was tired of this skulking about. I mean, this was the guy I was supposed to save, and I hadn't even talked to him yet. I had two reapers to help me, but one was distracted by her new toy, and the other was too entrenched in age-old protocol to try anything new.

"Just a minute more," Barnabas said for about the sixth time. "I want to see what he's doing."

From the shadows, Nakita looked at the back of her camera, the glow lighting her face as she grumbled, "He's a human, killing time. Time to kill the human."

Barnabas scowled at her from under his mop of curls, and I sighed.

I didn't like spying, and I stood between the bushes and the siding, thinking about bugs as I pushed my damp hair behind my ear and looked out over the dark yard. The neighborhood was a nice one—nicer than mine—and I wondered why a guy who had everything felt the need to take everything away from someone else.

The stars showed sharp past the outlines of roofs, and I worried that Ron might show up. Barnabas or Nakita had been hiding my amulet's resonance since we'd left my backyard. I probably should invest some time into learning how to do it myself. I didn't like relying on Barnabas or Nakita.

A burst of keyboard clatter drew my attention, and I peeked around the edge of the window to see Shoe still hunched at his computer. The guy's room was boring, with pale white walls and gray carpet that looked like it belonged in a doctor's office. His desk was scary-clean. Everything was on a shelf or tucked in a drawer. There were no clothes or clutter lying around. Even his bed was made. Apart from the Harvard banner, the only color was Ace's artwork. There were several music CDs on the tidy desk, and one big picture of swirling eagles with vicious talons taped to the closet door. Maybe his mother had a thing about thumbtacks in the wall. His music was boring, and I fiddled with the tips of my purple hair as the New Age nothing made me sleepy. Me, sleepy . . . and I hadn't had a good nap since I'd died.

"This is what you do on a reap?" I said, glancing down at Barnabas. "Spy on people?"

"I spot 'em and stick 'em," Nakita said, rustling the bushes as she came closer.

Eyes never leaving Shoe, Barnabas slid over to make room for her. "It's a reap prevention, not a reap," he said softly. "I'm not sure what to do, and there's nothing wrong with watching until we get an idea."

A soft sound, almost a growl, slipped from Nakita as she put her back to the house. "There are a hundred possible accidents in that room," she said. "I can make it look as if his power cord frayed and he electrocuted himself."

"No!" both Barnabas and I exclaimed softly.

Shoe looked up from his keyboard, hearing us maybe. I

dropped back and Barnabas dragged Nakita off to the other side. The sleepy music grew louder, but it wasn't until the clack of keys resumed that we relaxed and looked around the window again.

"You are not going to kill him!" Barnabas said, and she put her camera in her purse, frowning as she zipped it up.

"You have no idea how good I'm being," Nakita whispered, watching Shoe hit the print button, then lean to catch the paper as it shot out. "Chronos could have followed us here. If I get one whiff of him, I swear, I'm going to kill him."

Who, Ron or Shoe? I thought, eyeing Shoe. The guy was a total geek, but that didn't make him scythe-worthy. What the seraphs claimed just didn't fit with what I'd seen tonight. I'd watched him help his younger brother with a handheld game earlier, and he hadn't taken it away to show him what to do—instead, he walked the ten-year-old through the problem.

"I'd like to see you try," Barnabas said, not shifting his gaze from Shoe's room.

Nakita huffed, and I rolled my eyes. *Not again* . . . "You can't stop me," she said haughtily, a little too loudly for my liking. "This is what we do. Get used to it or leave. You're the new angel here. Not me."

Barnabas turned, his expression peeved. "That's a good idea," he said sourly. "Kill Shoe and blow to stardust Madison's chance to do things her way."

Her eyes narrowed. "Ron could be watching us right now.

I'm not going to let him put a guardian angel on Shoe!"

Oh, ma-a-a-an. They were going to make enough noise to bring Shoe to the window. It wasn't the introduction I really wanted. "Actually," I said before Barnabas could come back with anything, "Nakita has a valid concern."

The leaves rustled, and Barnabas turned to me. "What?"

Not meeting his eyes, I looked up at Nakita. "Why don't you make a couple of circles to make sure Ron or Paul isn't watching us?"

Barnabas hid his smile a shade too late. Nakita saw it, and she stiffened. "You're getting rid of me," she accused.

"Well, yeah," I said, not wanting to lie to her. She'd been lied to enough. "But you're right. Someone should keep watch. I pick you."

Her brow furrowed, and as her eyes shifted to silver for an instant, she said, "Fine," and stalked away.

I exhaled, rubbing the back of my neck in a show of nervous relief as she found her wings, and, with a downward thrust that sent grass clippings flying, she put herself in the air.

Barnabas stood and stretched. "Does 'fine' mean the same thing when Nakita says it as when you do?"

"Yup." Glancing back at Shoe, I felt a moment of uselessness. "He's just filling out college applications. Barnabas, Shoe is as exciting as oatmeal. Are you sure we're watching the right person? Even if he is a computer genius, he doesn't seem the kind of guy who's after anonymous notoriety by killing people."

Barnabas eased closer, and the scent of the back side of the clouds slid over me. "Think so?" he whispered. "He's bringing up a hidden folder."

Suddenly a lot more interested, I looked in to find Shoe still sitting at his computer. Squinting, I read, OPERATION VACATION, at the top of the new window. "Sounds innocuous enough," I said softly.

Barnabas rumbled deep in his chest, shifting his weight to his other foot. "Remember what Grace said? The school's computer is infected first. Vacation? As in shutting down the school and gaining a day or two off?"

Ooooooh, not good. Still, I wasn't convinced, even as Shoe popped one of Ace's decorated CDs into the laptop. "I've got to talk to him. Now."

Barnabas turned to me with wide eyes. "Did you see that?" he asked. "The disc had a black wing on it!"

He looked shocked, and I waved a hand in dismissal. "Sorry. I meant to tell you. It's Ace," I said, sending my gaze back into the gray and white bedroom. "He's an artist. Isn't it creepy? He got the idea for the melting crow from Shoe."

"'Creepy' is not the word I'd use," Barnabas grumped, resettling himself.

I watched as Shoe leaned back in his chair as the disc burned. Why he didn't put it on a jump drive escaped me. Maybe he was going to sneak it into school disguised as music?

Why am I still sitting here? I asked myself suddenly. He was loading the virus. What did I need to see him do? Plug it in?

"I'm going to talk to him," I said, gathering myself and pushing through the bushes to get to the front yard.

The branches scraped against my arms, and I halted when a pair of headlights lit the quiet street. They looked . . . blue. Not the headlights themselves, but the light.

"Hold up," Barnabas whispered as he pushed out to stand beside me, but I felt dizzy and I had already stopped, squinting when the headlights resolved into Ace's truck parked on the street. His loud music cut off three seconds after the engine did, and his door made a hard slam of sound. Footsteps soft, his shadowy form came around the front of the truck and headed for the walk.

"Ace," I said, holding my stomach. I felt queasy. We couldn't see the front door from where we were, but it was easy enough to follow his fast pace up the walk and then hear the cheerful dinging of the doorbell.

From Shoe's room came a muttered curse. Barnabas drew me behind a tree, and together we watched Shoe fidget, standing before his computer and almost falling when he tried to put on his shoes. "Hurry up!" he muttered as the drive still hummed. My eyes weren't working right, and I blinked, trying to get the haze of blue out of them. Glancing down at my amulet, I wondered if the silver mesh cradling it looked blue, too, or if it was my imagination.

Barnabas tightened his grip on my arm. "We have to go," he

said, eyes on the window.

"Why?" I asked, trying to shake a new buzzing from my ears.

He turned to me, his brown eyes holding a bothered impatience. "Because I think Shoe is going to come out the window as soon as that computer finishes."

Sure enough, Shoe had a black hoodie on, and was standing at the screen and fiddling with the little clips that held it in place. From outside, I could hear his mom at the door, inviting Ace in. Grimacing, I ducked behind the tree and out of sight.

The sound of wind among feathers brought our attention up, and I wasn't surprised to see Nakita lightly land on the roof. "Stay there!" Barnabas all but hissed at her, and the dark reaper grinned at him, making me shiver at her fierce expression. My eyes widened when she flipped him off, then jumped back into the air so she could follow Shoe, who was clearly going to go AWOL.

From inside, I heard Shoe's mom call for him. This was going to get ugly really fast.

"Does Nakita even know what that means?" I asked, putting a hand to my chest. *Why isn't my heart beating? It always beats when I get nervous.*

Barnabas pulled me back behind the tree. "I don't think so," he said, and I blinked up at him. His eyes were all silver. "We've got to go."

Everything is turning blue, I thought. I felt numb, indistinct.

Shoe finally got the screen off, and it scraped the window as he tucked it outside. His curtains fluttered as he closed them to hide the open window.

"We have to get out of here," Barnabas said, and he darted off across the grass.

I took a breath and pushed myself into motion. If not for the wind against my face, I wouldn't have been able to tell I was even moving. It was like a dream where you run and run, and you never go anywhere.

"Madison!" Barnabas called from the sidewalk, and I stopped. Blinking, I looked down. I was still beside the tree. *Wait a moment.* I knew I had run . . . somewhere.

"Madison, let's go!" Barnabas repeated, and I wavered. "He's going to come out!"

"I don't feel so good," I said, squinting at him.

And then the light from the street suddenly went entirely blue. Like ink falling into a glass of water, it poured from the middle, hitting the ground and rebounding against the sides of the beam of light, white and blue swirling until it was all one color.

Oh, this can't be good.

"Ummm," I breathed as Barnabas jogged back and took my arm. "I think I'm in trouble," I said. Then my knees gave way, and I collapsed.

"Madison!"

Head lolling, I felt Barnabas catch me. "Gabriel's pearly

toes," he muttered, and I opened my eyes. His face was glowing like you see in the movies, with a white smudginess. And I could see his wings. Reaching out, I tried to touch them, finding they were only in my vision, not real. He looked like the angel he was, fallen from grace. He was the only real thing left. Everything else was blue, sliding together into one monotone color of existence.

"Barnabas," I whispered, needing a huge breath to do it. "Something is wrong."

"You think?" he said, sounding panicked as he lifted me up into his arms. "What's the matter? Are you hurt?"

My gaze fell on my amulet, and I stared in wonder. It was absolutely black. No, it was a violet so deep that it only looked black. With a sudden understanding, I realized it had gone ultraviolet, the color falling off the visible spectrum.

My head lolled up, and I gasped as I saw the stars. They were rainbows of noncolors. I could see all the wavelengths blaring from them, and I started to cry. It was too much. I was only human. I wasn't supposed to see all of this, to even know such colors existed.

"Madison!"

Barnabas turned my face from the heavens, and, sobbing, I gripped him as if he were the only thing real. "Something is . . . wrong," I stammered. I wanted to look again, but couldn't bear it.

"I'll find Ron," Barnabas said. His voice was grim, and

though a wave of dizziness hit me, I focused on him.

"No," I breathed, then louder, "No! Just don't let me look at the stars." I was crying, and I could see waves of blue coming from me, bouncing into him like waves on a beach. "Don't let me look at the stars . . ." I whispered. And as Barnabas panicked, I felt my mind expand.

Like blowing out a flame, he dissolved into a blue puff of smoke and vanished. That fast, I was alone, and all that held me sane was the glow of his aura beside mine as I found myself entirely within the fabric of time.

Eight

Where the devil am I? I thought, watching my fingers move as if through a blue haze as I grabbed the back of a rolling chair and swung it to face the computer before me. *Holy cow, I'm in Shoe's room! And those don't actually look like my fingers. . . .*

"See how you like it," I felt my lips say; then I heard it an instant later, masculine and ticked.

Crap! I'm in Shoe? I thought, but I had sat down, or Shoe had, rather, and I turned my head without wanting to in order to make sure the door was shut. Leaning back in the chair, I looked at the closed curtains. A faint musing intruded in my thoughts that I'd seen someone out there, running away.

Barnabas and me, I thought as I looked at hands that weren't mine, but clearly Shoe couldn't sense me as I could sense him. It was freaky, and I didn't like the blue tint everything had. I could hear his heartbeat and feel his breath in him, sensing it go stale an instant before he exhaled. His foot itched in his shoe, and it was driving me nuts that he didn't scratch it. I was hot and irritable, and for the first time in months, I remembered what it was to be hungry.

I'm flashing forward, I thought, the memory of adrenaline washing through me to mix with Shoe's anger. *An instant before it happens.*

"This is going to be good," I heard Shoe mutter as he leaned forward and tapped his fingers on the desk in a fast rhythm. "No one will be able to prove it was me. I'm smarter than all you lamebrains think."

My fingers were stiff as the tapping turned into a smack on the desk. "God, this computer is slow," I heard myself mutter, feeing an emotion of irritation that wasn't mine.

Shoe, no! You're going to kill people! I thought, trying to get him to hear me, but without any indication that he'd sensed me, he stood and put his ear to the door, listening for Ace.

Damn it, I knew it wouldn't be that easy, but I could feel the desperation growing in both of us as I watched everything happen, unable to stop it, unable to make myself be heard in his head.

Agitated, Shoe chewed on a fingernail as the drive hummed. *Clean, clean, everything has to be so friggin' clean,* I heard him think as he scraped the ink out from under his nail, then flicked it to the middle of the room. *I've got to get out of here,* came echoing into our shared mind.

Shoe, stop! I thought, screaming into his brain, but he stood before the computer and shoved the chair back and fidgeted, waiting. *God! Could the piece of crap be any slower?*

Finally the disc finished and the drawer slid open. I reached for it, and though I couldn't see it, I knew he was smiling at the image of the dripping black bird. He jammed it into a back pocket, and a flood of emotion slipped into me.

He was so out of here. He'd known him his entire life, and this was how he was treated? They'd all know tomorrow at school. He'd be sure everyone knew who was responsible for everything. And his so-called friend could curl up and die, for all he cared.

Shoe! I exclaimed, but a heavier wash of tinted blue obscured my vision.

The world seemed to turn inside out, and I floundered. Again I was lost in the black fabric of time, lit from the bright line of a million conscious thoughts. A flash of blue intruded, and with a pinpoint of explosion, I was back. Sort of.

I don't feel so good, I thought, and then a wave of satisfaction I didn't know the source of swallowed everything else. I couldn't see anything. A blue so deep it was almost black hazed my vision until that was all there was, but I knew I was in someone's mind. They were comfortable, and I could feel a heartbeat . . . smell food. My fingers were greasy, and I felt a pang of hunger when I realized I was eating something salty.

As if coming through a blanket, I could hear a TV sitcom, the only thing clear being the laugh track. Behind it was a woman's voice, the sound of the pauses and hesitations making me think she was on the phone.

"No," she said. "They won't let anyone in, especially the volunteers. They're the top suspects, but the entire hospital is under investigation."

I felt my chest move as I chuckled, a flush of satisfaction making me both happy and angry. Shoe was pleased, but I was mad. Not that he could tell.

But this hasn't happened yet, I thought, thinking I must be farther out into the future, because the only thing that was clear were voices. That and my hunger. Man, I'd missed that, and my mouth watered as I felt myself crunch down on a chip.

"No!" the woman said, sounding appalled. "Three people died. It took them an unreal four hours to even know they had a problem. They could have lost twice that many. They think maybe it's a disgruntled employee. The firewall didn't catch it because someone *put* it there. It wasn't through the internet."

Shoe, you are slime, I thought as he chuckled, shoving chips into his mouth and turning the TV down so he could hear better. I couldn't see the remote, but I could feel it. And why was it that sound traveled better through time than vision?

"Yes, an inside job," the woman was saying. "And they're going to get the little perp."

Instead of fear, I felt pleasure. It was all Shoe, of course, and

I tried to give him a headache. Here I thought he was an okay guy, but being in his head had cured me of that.

"They've got the disc," she said. "Tracked it to the terminal it came in on. All they need to do now is match it to the computer that burned it. Isn't that something?" she said loudly. "Yes, they can do that. Like matching the ballistics of a bullet. They're only interviewing people right now, but the search warrants will come. You know they will. The idiot put a label on it. It might be a kid, since the same thing happened at the school yesterday."

My lips moved, and I heard a whispered, "Ooooh, I'm gonna get your ass busted."

Shoe! I exclaimed into my mind, but it was only a dream, a possibility—it hadn't even happened yet—and I felt a surge of frustration when every single sound cycled down to a pinpoint of bluish black until there was nothing, no voices, no touch . . . nothing.

For an instant I hung there, not knowing what was going to happen next.

And then I gasped as the world flashed red.

I jerked. My arm smacked into something, and I heard Barnabas grunt. Scared, I opened my eyes. I had eyes, and they opened when I wanted them to. *Thank God.* It was over.

Barnabas was looking down at me. He was close, really close. Above him was the smooth, unmistakable roof of a car. The muffled stillness of being shut in pressed against my ears.

"Uh," I stammered, thinking he looked terrified. "Why are you holding me?"

His mouth dropped open, and his eyes flashed silver for a second. "Stars to dust, what happened?" he said as his grip on me loosened. "Are you okay?"

He let me slip to the seat beside him, and I sat up, shaking as I brushed the purple tips of my hair out of my eyes. We were in the backseat of a van, and it looked like we were still in Shoe's neighborhood. Holding a hand to my stomach, I glanced at Barnabas and remembered his wings. They weren't there now, but maybe they were just an instant before or behind us in time. Before the now and the next? I almost thought I could see them if I squinted.

"Everything went blue," I said. "Where are we?"

Barnabas exhaled softly and wiped a hand across his forehead. "Someone's van," he said, shifting his shoulders as if trying to relax. "It was open. You were crying about the stars. Once you couldn't see them, you calmed down—somewhat. Madison, what happened? You just went all stiff."

I touched my face, realizing it was wet. Unable to look at him, I wiped it off. "You've never seen anyone do that before?" I asked, seeing my hand shake. The two red stripes on my fingernails looked funny. "Ron, maybe?"

From the corner of my sight, I watched him shake his head. "You scared the ever-loving feather dust out of me. I've never . . . I've never even heard of . . . What happened?"

I couldn't tell if I was hungry or if I was going to be sick. I felt like I hadn't eaten in weeks. And I hadn't. "I think it was a flash forward," I said, thinking, *This is my job? I'm going to do this how often?* I had to find my body, like, yesterday. "Everything went blue, and I could see your wings," I finished, feeling ill.

Barnabas cleared his throat. "Why would seeing the stars hurt?"

Turning to him, I shrugged. I honestly couldn't remember. It was as if my mind had blocked it out. Maybe the human mind couldn't take that much beauty. "I don't know," I said softly. "But, Barnabas, I watched Shoe uploading the virus into a computer disc. I was him, but he couldn't hear me, even when I told him to stop. Then things shifted, and I felt his satisfaction when he heard about the people dying at the hospital. The guy is whacked! I don't understand it. He looks so normal."

"No wonder Ron never said anything about his flash forwards," Barnabas said, his brown eyes holding heavy concern. "Madison, it was awful. It was as if you weren't all there. I thought if I let you go, you might . . . vanish. Like your being dead took away your anchor to get back. Your amulet wasn't keeping you grounded to the time lines. I was."

Fear slid through me. "Were there black wings?"

His shook his head, but the look in his eyes scared me. "No. But I thought if I let you go, you'd be gone," he said. "I'm supposed to be keeping you safe. I've never been that terrified."

His lips parted as he searched for words, and I swear, if I had a heart, it would have skipped a beat at the worry in his eyes. "And you're going to do it again."

Frightened, I swallowed and looked at the fast-food child's-meal toy on the floor, not knowing if I believed him about the black wings. What if this happened while I was at school? They'd put me on meds or something.

"It will be okay," I said, shuddering. "I know what flashing forward feels like now. Before it happened, all the light went blue. Next time, I'll just find a quiet room or something."

"Blue. Like you were moving faster in time," Barnabas said, seeming to find comfort in that there would be some warning.

A sudden thought pulled me straight, my own fear vanishing as I tossed the hair from my eyes. "And if I've flashed forward, then maybe Ron did, too." Crap, if he saw what I had seen, he'd know who the mark was. I stood, almost hitting my head on the ceiling. "We have to go," I said, feeling light-headed and weak. I'd not been hungry or ill for months, and being that way now was a shock. Maybe flashing forward had taken a lot out of my amulet.

"Where's Nakita?" I asked when he didn't move, still sitting on the van's bench seat and looking at me as if I were going to break apart. "If I saw the future, then Shoe has made his decision, and his fate is set unless I can change his mind. I've got to talk to him before he does something stupid or Ron IDs him."

Barnabas took my arm, drawing me back. "Madison, slow

down. You're not well."

"I'll be fine," I said, feeling shaky as I tugged on the door and it didn't move. "But Ron can tell who the mark is now. He sees what I see, right? If we don't find Shoe before whatever light reaper Ron sends out does, Nakita will kill him. Barnabas, I've run out of time!"

The irony of that wasn't lost on me, and I tugged on the latch, but either I wasn't doing it right or it had a child lock on it. Huffing in impatience, I leaned back in the seat and said, "Some help here, please?"

Silent and grim faced, he reached across me and pulled the door open. I'd been doing it right; I was just too weak.

I stumbled when I jumped to the curb, and I couldn't help but glance at the puddle of streetlight to reassure myself it was a cheerful yellow instead of an inky blue-black. "Where is the school from here?" I asked. *If she killed him, I'm going to be so pissed. I have not gone through this for nothing.*

"You'll never make it in time on foot," Barnabas said, and I gasped when he scooped me up, cradling me as he gave one downward thrust with his wings, and we were airborne.

Nine

Barnabas's arms were tight around me as he flew over what had to be the high school. While Nakita and I had been trying to pass my dad's spaghetti off on Josh, Barnabas had been canvassing the town of Fort Banks, a foresight I was now reaping the benefit of. The flat, pebbled roof with its big air-conditioning units was featureless in the dark. It smelled like tar, and the air grew warmer when he drifted over it and found the back of the school with its big expanse of parking lot.

"Do you see Nakita?" I asked, scanning for any sign of her, Shoe, or even Grace.

"No," he said softly, and I hoped we weren't too late.

"Do you think I should try calling her?" I asked, and he shifted the tilt of his wings to make us fly parallel to the rows of black windows along the side.

"I'd have to stop hiding your resonance and hope she is doing the same. Ron might hear," he said, finishing softly, "Better to just look."

"I suppose," I said, frustrated.

"No black wings," Barnabas said, making me think that there had been when I flashed forward, and he just hadn't told me.

"Yet," I said sourly. A darting motion attracted my attention, and I pointed. "There!" I said, but Barnabas had seen it, too. It was Shoe, halfway through a low window with one foot inside, one on the sill. Nakita was talking to him from outside, having probably surprised him. The faint, softball-size glow over her was likely Grace. The dark reaper didn't have her sword out, but I could tell by Grace's haze that things were not going well.

Barnabas angled away, and, startled, I yelled, "Where are you going?"

"I don't want him to see me with my wings," he said, and Grace, who had clearly heard me, darted up and our way.

"Barnabas, I'm trying to convince him he needs to change his life or risk being cut down by an angel. Land where he can freaking see you! You can always change his memory."

Making a grunt of understanding, he shifted his course, wings beating three times to cushion our landing on the pavement.

"He's here! You need to hurry!" Grace said, her haze looking dim against the stars as she flew in circles around us. My hair flew straight up from the gust of Barnabas's wings. "She chased him inside!"

I stumbled away from Barnabas as my feet found the earth, tugging my skirt down where it should be. Nakita had vaulted inside, but she was lingering by the window to watch Shoe and us both. Her sword was drawn, and I didn't need to see the future to know everything was about to crash down.

"Grace, tell her to wait!" I said. "Ron isn't here! We're okay!"

"Got it!" she sang out, and in a flash of silver she zoomed away.

Ron isn't *here, is he?* I questioned myself. Grace was. She'd been keeping an eye on Paul. Was she still, or had she shifted over to spy on me again? The seraphs were watching. *Nothing like a little pressure to bring out your best,* I thought, grimacing.

Barnabas came up beside me, and as we started forward, Nakita and Shoe vanished deeper inside the building.

"Damn it!" I shouted, not caring if God himself heard me. I was mad. I didn't feel very good from my flash forward. And now Nakita was going to scythe the Shoe and turn all our efforts into puppy presents on the rug.

I jogged toward the long rows of windows, gasping when I stumbled. Barnabas caught my elbow until I found my balance. The open window wasn't that far above the ground, but Barnabas unexpectedly boosted me up and, in a sliding sound of crashing chairs, I landed inside the school, arms and legs tangling.

This is so not cool, I thought, trying to get up and finally having to accept Barnabas's hand. But my ungraceful entrance had stopped everyone, and both Nakita and Shoe were staring at me instead of each other. Grace giggled while I adjusted my clothes and directed Barnabas with a nod to cover the second door into the hall. Somehow Nakita had gotten in front of Shoe and was blocking the first door. Grace, unseen by Shoe, hovered over him.

It was a chemistry lab, dark but for the light coming in from the outside security lights. There were six long benches with sinks and little spigots for the Bunsen burners. A skeleton grinned at me from the corner, and I stifled a shiver. "Nakita," I said, still embarrassed from my entrance. "Let me talk to him. I can save him."

"So can I," Nakita said as she shifted her feet to find her balance. "It will be a lot faster, too."

"I told her!" Grace chimed out. "She called me a firefly."

Shoe looked both angry and bewildered, and from the second door, Barnabas said loudly, "The seraphs have granted her a chance, Nakita. Let her try."

Feet spread wide, Nakita tossed her hair defiantly, but when Grace cleared her throat to make a sound like a wind chime, Nakita grudgingly added, "Talk to him, but if a black wing shows, I'm scything him."

"Scythe me?" Shoe was starting to look nervous as he eyed her sword. "What the hell are you doing? Who are you?"

"Madison is how she was christened," Grace sang merrily. "When she's angry her eyes tend to glisten. Lives she does save, no thanks does she crave. It'd be easier if you crapheads would listen."

Jeez, does she sit awake at night thinking these things up?

"Uh," I started, but Shoe was staring at me, finger pointed.

"You were at the mall," he accused. "You're that girl Ace was talking to. You like him?" Shoe relaxed into a cocky stance. "Go for it. He's an ass."

"No, it's you I wanted to talk to," I said, but he'd turned away.

"That's a new one," he said sourly as he started for Nakita and the door, only to stop short when she began swinging her sword.

"Talk to Madison, or I'll cut you down right now," she threatened.

"Nakita . . ." I complained.

But Shoe was backing up. "What is *wrong* with you?"

"Nothing," Grace said cheerfully. "She's here to help. Really!"

"One more step," Nakita begged him, her beautiful face going savage. "Just one more, and this farce of trying to change fate will be over. Talk to Madison. She's trying to save your worthless life. I'm simply trying to save your soul," she finished bitterly.

Clearly unnerved, Shoe glanced first at Barnabas by the back door, then at me by the open window. "Shoe," I said, capturing his attention. "I know about the virus."

"Yeah?" he said bitterly. "Ace talks too much."

"It's going to get out and shut down the hospital," I said, trying to keep him focused. "People are going to die."

Shoe shook his head, glancing at Nakita as she practiced a few swings. "Is that what Ace told you? The virus is a prank. A way for me to gain some notoriety in my last year as the guy who shut down school for a day. That's it. It can't get out, and it doesn't replicate. You're more stupid than your shoes look if you believe anything Ace tells you."

"There is nothing wrong with my shoes!" I said hotly, fist on my hip as Grace laughed. "And the virus kills people. I saw it!"

Shoe crossed his arms over his chest and put his weight on one foot. "You *saw* it? What are you? Some kind of teen-intervention mega enforcer? Am I on camera? Is this a joke or some weird reality-TV show?"

That was insulting, and I huffed.

"He's not listening, Madison," the dark reaper said, clearly eager to get on with it as her grip shifted. "This is why no one ever tries to reason with a mark. They don't listen. They never believe."

Frustrated, I rounded on her. "They don't believe because you don't show them anything to believe in!"

Barnabas had been inching closer to Nakita, and I felt as if things were spiraling out of control when he gripped his amulet and his scythe appeared. "I'm sorry, Madison," he said, his face taking on a grim expression. "I wanted this to work, but he's not going to listen, and I'm not going to let her kill Shoe."

Shoe's mouth dropped open, and his eyes widened, but Barnabas had his sword pointed at Nakita, not him. "He doesn't deserve to die," Barnabas said to her. "I bested you before, and I will again."

"You freaks are going to try to kill me?" Shoe said, his voice getting higher. "What the hell is wrong with you?"

Grace's wings seemed to dim. I wasn't too happy, either.

This was so getting out of control. The seraphs would never believe it was possible if I couldn't do this at least once. "Barnabas, put your scythe away!" I shouted. "Nakita, back off! You guys are driving me nuts! Neither of you is giving this a chance!"

Both of them lowered their swords, and I took a breath. Shoe swore softly, and I strode forward, ticked. He was going to listen, damn it. I didn't have time for this!

Knowing that everything that happened was going to land in a seraph's ear by way of Grace, I tried to calm myself, but it didn't work. "Look, you!" I said right in Shoe's face, to make him back up, startled. "I don't like Ace. And I don't particularly like you. Let's just say I have access to tomorrow's headlines, okay? The aliens beamed them down to me, all right? If Barnabas gets his way, the papers will read, 'Three dead in the hospital from a computer virus.' If Nakita gets her way, it's going to be your name in the obituaries to save your soul at the expense of your life. Me, I'm trying to do the impossible and have the headlines read, 'Average day in average America—everyone's happy.' But if you don't even try, I don't think I can stop Nakita from putting your head on a platter!"

Grace seemed to dim a little more. Barnabas made a pained-sounding noise, but I couldn't spare him a glance. I felt sick. This was not what I wanted to do. I had thought it would be so easy. Find the mark, talk to the mark, we all go home to be dead another day.

His face pale in the dim light, Shoe eyed the reapers, then shuddered when he looked at their swords. "Who are you?"

His voice lacked the earlier mockery, and, encouraged, I said, "The only person besides you who can fix this. Don't upload the virus. Please."

He swallowed hard, his gaze returning to Nakita before jerking back to me. Clearly he'd seen something in her that he couldn't explain, a glint of the eye, a gesture so graceful a human couldn't make it. A sense of the divine, perhaps. Finally he was listening. "Madison. They called you Madison," he said, attention coming back to me.

Sighing, I extended my hand, and Grace made a happy sound. "I'm Madison. Nice to meet you, Shoe." His hand in mine felt cold, and he let go almost immediately. "Listen to me," I said, noting that Nakita was looking at me like I'd done the impossible in getting him to pay attention. "Somehow the virus you made gets out. It messes up the hospital system. Three people die before they know what's going on. Just don't do it."

Outside, a dark shadow passed over the window. My gut tightened. Nakita had seen it, and her expression went empty as she slipped to the window to look out. *Black wings?*

Shoe glanced at the open door. "It's not that kind of virus," he repeated. "It won't get out, and it doesn't replicate. That's why I had to break into the school to upload it. I'm not a freak. I want the notoriety for getting everyone a day off from school, not killing people. What kind of monster do you think I am?"

"The kind whom Nakita tries to kill," Barnabas said, but something in Shoe's words had struck me.

"You *had* to break in to upload it?" I whispered, hearing the past tense he had put everything in. My eyes pinched, I looked at him. "You already uploaded it," I said, and Nakita pulled back from the window while Grace sighed loudly enough for me to hear. "You were coming out of the school when Nakita found you, not going in."

"Well, yeah," he said, shrugging. "It's done. It's already in. When the clock ticks over to six in the morning, the system will shut down. Fire, security, everything. But that's all that's going to happen. It can't get out!"

Nakita strode forward, her face ugly. My eyes widened. Shoe darted for the door, and I grabbed his arm, swinging him behind me. If he ran, it would be over.

"Look out!" Grace shrilled, and I ducked.

Nakita's sword struck Barnabas's, inches before me. Damn it, I had to work harder in figuring out how to make a sword from my amulet. This relying on Barnabas was getting old.

"Knock it off!" I shouted as I rose out of my crouch, grateful that Barnabas could move that fast.

"You're crazy!" Shoe was yelling behind me. "Crazy! All of you!"

From the ceiling, Grace chimed in merrily, "Nakita, a reaper of light, the bad guy she wanted to smite. But Barney had planned, to make a big stand, to draw lines between wrong and the right."

Nakita's face went livid.

"Stop it! All of you!" I exclaimed. "This is my scything, not yours!"

The two reapers stared at each other, the air smelling of ozone. I could almost see their wings. As if in slow motion, they lowered their swords and stepped away from each other. Shaking, I turned to Shoe. That flash forward had really taken it out of me. "Sorry," I said, wondering if he still had the ability to listen after that. "Nakita is intense."

"She's freaking crazy!" he shouted, then shivered when Grace landed on his shoulder, bathing him in a glow he couldn't see.

"He said it's too late," Nakita said, trying to defend her actions.

Choice—it was never too late to make a new one. "It's not

too late," I said, giving Barnabas a thankful look. "We can take the virus out. Shoe, you've got a patch, yes?"

"Yes," he admitted, looking darkly at Nakita. "But I'm telling you, the virus won't spread. It can't." Reaching to his back pocket, he brought out the disc. "This won't do anything but shut the school down!"

I took a breath to disagree, but when I saw the disc decorated with Ace's artwork, a cold feeling trickled through me. The disc in Shoe's hand wasn't the disc I'd seen in my flash forward. *Crap on toast, how stupid can I be?*

Oblivious as to why I was staring at the disc, Barnabas drew close. "Madison, I'm sorry," he was saying, but I wasn't listening. "Maybe if we had been faster."

With a thump, my pulse staggered into play. *How am I going to fix this?* "That isn't the same disc I saw in the flash forward," I said, panic making my voice sound thin.

Nakita's head came up, and her grip on her sword tightened. Grace made a sound like bells, and her glow went completely out. "She flashed forward?" Nakita asked Barnabas, then looked at me. "You flashed forward? Then he's the mark!"

I shook my head, cursing myself for assuming I'd been in Shoe's mind when I'd found myself in his room. "No," I whispered, a hand to my stomach. Fumbling, I took the disc from Shoe and waved it under Barnabas's nose. "This isn't the disc I saw in the flash. It has Ace's artwork on it, but it's not the same disc. Shoe isn't the mark."

Nakita was ashen. "I almost scythed him. I . . . would have."

"It's my fault," I said. Everything was blue when I saw the virus being uploaded to the disc. It was Ace. I'd been in Ace while he made a duplicate of the virus in Shoe's computer. Maybe the future wasn't here yet. Why hadn't I tried to get him to look in a mirror?

As if from a great distance, I heard Barnabas say, "We're following the wrong person."

"It's Ace," I said, as if it weren't already crystal clear, and Shoe jerked back when I grabbed his hand, looking at his fingertips. "There's no ink on your hands."

"What is your problem?" he asked, pulling back out of my grip.

"My problem is that I'm stupid!" I exclaimed, taking a step forward and feeling faint. "I'm such a dunce! Shoe, I saw Ace in your room at your computer. I thought it was you. He downloaded the virus to a disc. We have to find Ace before Ron does."

"You were spying on me?" Shoe said hotly, and I grimaced. He was worried about a little spying?

"Ace is trying to get even with you. I thought I was seeing *you* be mad at *him*. I never considered it might be him mad at you." I had to find Ace. He was somewhere with that virus.

"He's been mad at me for a long time," Shoe said softly. "He knew I was doing this tonight, and now I bet he's going to make it look like I downed the hospital, too. I ought to kill him."

Nakita dissolved her sword in a flashy show of whirling. "No need. I'll do it."

Shoe's face went pale. "I was kidding."

"I'm not."

"Life ended, a soul to save," Grace said mournfully. "Decisions age-old are made. Is it choice? Is it fate? Forgiveness or hate? When love is what all of us crave."

Shocked, I stared at her dim glow. It was . . . good.

Barnabas touched my arm, and I jerked. "Ace's mother works at the hospital," he reminded me, and I turned to the black windows.

Nakita leaned to look out at the sky, her long throat showing in the light. "He has a way to get in."

Beside me, Shoe was clenching his teeth. "And he knows how to upload it. I showed him how. I'm such an idiot. I'm going to get blamed for this, not him."

Stomach knotting, I looked at Barnabas. "We have to get to the hospital."

At the window, Nakita made a muffled oath, then shouted, "Drop!"

I stared at the window, seeing the black shape coming at it. Barnabas reached up and yanked me down behind one of the lab stations. I hit Shoe on the way, and he fell under me. "Hey!" I yelped, then clapped my hands over my ears as something crashed through the window.

Glass flew, tinkling, and a faint bell began ringing. *Swell. Just peachy keen.*

"It's Ron!" Grace chimed out, her hazy shadow darting over us.

I picked a piece of glass out of my hair and sat up, safe behind the tall lab bench. "No kidding."

From inside the room came Ron's harrumph, and I could almost see him standing with his feet spread wide and his eyes turning blue like they did when he was angry. At least he wasn't trying to stop time. "Madison!" he said loudly, and I met Shoe's eyes, mouthing for him to stay down. "It's over. I'm putting a guardian angel on him."

I peeked above the lab bench to find Ron at the front of the room before the whiteboard. A hazy glow above him had to be the guardian angel, as yet unassigned. Ron was wearing his usual off-white tunic and pants, and he looked satisfied. It was all I could do to keep my mouth shut and let him believe that Shoe was the mark. *Maybe I can pull this off after all.*

"Go," Barnabas said, hunched beside me. "Grace and I will keep him busy. If he wants to put an angel on Shoe, then Ace doesn't have one yet."

"Madison?" Ron called. "Show yourself."

"But you can't stand up to Ron!" I almost hissed. "He'll just stop time or something."

Grace drifted down to land on Barnabas's shoulder, giggling. "I'm a guardian angel first, baby," she said, her words cheerful.

"I can keep Ron from messing with time."

"We'll be fine," Barnabas said, gesturing with his eyes for me to leave. "Go."

"What about the other guardian angel?" I asked.

"She doesn't have free will," Grace said. "No name, you see."

I licked my lips, wondering if I might be able to salvage something. Shoe's life, maybe.

"Madison! Come out and admit you lost!" Ron shouted. "There's no shame here. You can't expect to win when you're trying to beat a thousand years of experience."

This guy has an ego bigger than my old chemistry teacher's.

"Go!" Barnabas said urgently as Shoe stared at us, frightened. "Nakita, you go with them. In case you have to . . ."

His words trailed off, and I met his eyes, shocked. Was he agreeing with Nakita's position, to kill Ace if he wouldn't change?

Nakita, too, was surprised. "You think I'm right in ending his life?" she asked, and Shoe fidgeted, seeming more concerned about not getting caught in a demolished lab than with our conversation about killing his friend.

"No. I mean, I don't know what I believe anymore," Barnabas said, his brown eyes solemn. "I held Madison as she lived in the shadows of the future, heard her cry from the pain of the beauty in the stars. Maybe it would be better if his life ended before he does himself so large a hurt and robs his soul of the chance to find that beauty. I don't . . . know anymore. I have . . .

doubt." His eyes came to mine. "Please make him see reason. Don't force me to have to make that choice."

I swallowed, scared. Were things so wrong that an angel doubted his own mind?

"Madison!" Ron shouted.

Nakita touched Barnabas's arm. "I understand," she said softly.

From above us, Grace said, "Uh, guys? He's coming over here."

Barnabas looked at all of us in turn. "On the count of three," he said, then took a breath. "One. Two—"

"Three!" Nakita shouted, jumping straight up to land atop the bench, screaming as she drew her sword. On her chest, her amulet glowed a sharp amethyst, hurting my eyes.

"Nakita!" Ron exclaimed, and Grace lit up, bathing Nakita in a crystalline beauty. My amulet warmed, and I knew the former guardian angel was blocking whatever Ron was trying to do as Nakita screamed at him, her sword making large circles as she advanced.

Barnabas sighed and hunched closer. "Three," he said. "Get Shoe out of here. Talk to Ace. Please make him understand. We'll catch up with you."

It was all the encouragement I needed. Grabbing Shoe's hand, I ran, trying to stay below the level of the benches. Glass sparkled on the floor, and the night air came in through the broken windows. Cars had pulled up, and flashing lights had begun playing on the ceilings.

Cop cars and alarm bells. Ohhh, I knew this song. We had to leave, and leave now. Ron's breaking of the window had been more than noticed.

"What about her?" Shoe said when we skittered out of the room and into the hall. It was cooler out here, and darker.

I glanced behind us and sighed. "Nakita doesn't want to kill you now. She's after Ace. You'll be fine."

Breaking into a jog, we headed down the hall. "I got that part. Is she coming?"

It never failed to amaze me how people could go from fear to acceptance. Meeting him stride for stride, I said, "She'll catch up. How did you get here? Will your bike hold two?"

Shoe pulled me into a room. It was another lab, and, moving fast, he led me to the back and the attached greenhouse. "I've got a car. But with the cops—"

"A car?" I interrupted him. "How do you sneak out your bedroom window, then drive a car to the school?" For all my moaning and groaning about having left my car in Florida, I'd found a new freedom with my bike. Slipping away was easier when you weren't making noise.

"I park it in the street," he said, flashing me a grin. "It's not like my parents want it in the drive. They can't get their cars out with me in the way."

I nodded as Shoe pointed to an open window in the school's greenhouse.

Another boom shook the school, followed by the sound of frantic radio chatter. The hoot of the fire alarm started. An instant later, the sprinklers went off.

"Damn!" Shoe said, watching the water spill out of the ceiling. There weren't any spigots in the greenhouse, and, glad for small favors, I bent to slip out the narrow window. I could hear cops in the hallways complaining about the water. I'd be willing to bet that between Ron and Barnabas, everyone in the school with a pulse would remember tonight just as the one when the fire alarm went off.

My feet skidded on the dew-wet grass when I finally got outside. The night was cool, and I waited, fidgeting and scanning the empty parking lot while Shoe scraped himself out the window. There was a glow on the horizon where the moon was about to rise. Shoe's feet thumped silently onto the grass, and after a quick look at the distant cop lights, we jogged across the empty parking lot.

"So where's your car?" I asked, hoping Barnabas and Nakita were being enough of a distraction, but not so big that it made international news.

"I didn't want it seen at the school, so I parked it down the street," he said, breathless as we ran. But when we rounded the corner, it was me who stopped dead in my tracks.

Shoe drove a gray convertible. And the top was down.

"No freaking way," I said, the memory of my heart pounding in a past fear. It looked like the car I had died in. Right down to the leather seats and the key in the ignition.

Shoe jumped over the closed door and turned the key. "Get in!" he exclaimed, surprised to find me six feet back. Behind me, fire trucks were starting to arrive.

I can do this, I thought, carefully opening the door and getting in. *It's not the same car. It's not the same driver.* But the thudding of my heart seemed real enough to shake even the illusion of my body. "Put your seat belt on," I said as I settled into the rich leather seats as if I were glass and could break.

"We're only going a couple of miles," he griped, looking over his shoulder as he backed up, the lights of the cop cars a distant threat.

"Put your seat belt on!" I yelled, and his eyes widened, black in the dim light.

"Okay, okay!" he said, and I glared at him until he did. "Freaky girl."

"I died in a car just like this," I said to try to explain myself, then laughed nervously. "Just kidding." He'd probably stop believing me if *he* thought *I* thought I was dead.

He gripped the wheel tighter, not saying anything as he got us on the road and away from the commotion at the school. It wasn't until we'd gone about a quarter mile that he flicked on the lights, and I breathed easier. "We need to stop at your place and get the patch," I said, holding my hair out of my face. "Ace might still be there. I don't know how far into the future I saw that first time."

Oooooh, I thought, biting my tongue as I realized what I had just said. That was going to be hard to laugh off.

Shoe stared at me as he drove. "Future?" he said softly, as though this was just sinking in, and I winced.

"Can you, um, ignore that last part?" I asked him, and he looked scared.

Anxious and jittery, I closed my mouth before I told him anything that would make him want to kick me out of the car. I still had a chance. It wasn't too late. I had to make this work. It wasn't just Ace's future on the line. It was my own.

Ten

Shoe parked two houses down from his on the other side of the street, frowning at Ace's truck still at the curb. Getting out without opening the car doors, we ran up the sidewalk, slowing as we neared. Shoe wasn't in very good shape, even as skinny as he was. The almost full moon had finally risen, helping light the black yards. Ace's truck was ticking as we passed it, the big engine still cooling. Maybe we were in time. Maybe nothing I'd seen in my flash forward had happened yet.

"You aren't even breathing hard," Shoe said, puffing.

"Yeah, well, I run a lot." Fidgeting at the slower pace, I shivered, thinking it odd that I felt cold at all. "How long will it take to get the patch?" I asked.

Shoe glanced at me. "It will take longer to introduce you to my mom."

The toes of my sneakers grew wet with the dew, and I glanced at Shoe's room. The light was shifting as someone inside moved around. *Ace?* "Your mom thinks you're still in your room," I reminded him, thinking he must not go AWOL often.

Shoe immediately shifted direction. "The window it is, then."

I couldn't help my smile at his slight frown. He wasn't very good at this sneaking-around thing, even if he had the car routine down. But his frown turned into anger when we got closer and we saw Ace messing around in Shoe's top desk drawer. "What is he doing?" Shoe whispered angrily, but I was elated. We were in time.

"I don't know. Maybe he hasn't downloaded the virus to the hospital yet," I said.

Shoe's brow furrowed, and with an awkward motion he gripped the sill and swung himself up and in. "Get the hell out of my desk," he said as he tugged his black hoodie straight.

Ace spun, his shock clear. His startled gaze shifted past Shoe to me as I came in, and his eyes narrowed. "Hey, Shoe," he huffed, shoving the drawer shut and backing away. "You owe me a five. I was just looking for it."

"Right," Shoe mocked, shoving him from his desk with a single open hand. Head down, Shoe pulled the drawer open as Ace caught his balance. Shoe sifted through the clutter. His eyes widening, he looked at me as if he didn't believe it, then tossed a laminated card to the desktop. "That's your mom's," he said, and my lips parted at the hospital ID. I hadn't seen *that* in my flash forward. "What are you doing, Ace?"

Instead of being angry, Ace rocked back with a satisfied expression. "Yeah, it's my mom's, and now it's got your fingerprints all over it. Dumb ass."

Shoe fisted his hands, coming forward a step. "You want to put it in the hospital? Are you crazy? Someone might get hurt. Give me the disc."

Smirking, Ace sat on his bed, casual and infuriating in his black T-shirt, which was too thin to hide how skinny he was. "Too late. It's already in."

Too late? Had Ace been to the hospital already?

"You are a friggin' idiot!" Shoe exploded, and I wished he'd tone it down. "All we wanted was the day off. Some notoriety. It's a hospital, Ace! You're going to kill someone! What's wrong with you?"

Ace stood, and I took a step back at his ugly expression. "What's wrong with me? What's wrong with you? This is your fault. You're ditching me, and you're gonna take your hit like a man. It's your computer. I don't know nothing about it."

Shoe shook his head, aghast. "This is because I'm going to *college*? What do you want me to do? Marry you? People grow up! Move away! I'm going to college, not the moon! You could go, too, if you wanted!"

I heard a soft click of heels outside the door, and I felt scared. But Shoe's mother was walking away, letting them take care of their issues on their own. She clearly wasn't ignorant of their friendship being on the skids.

Ace's expression was ugly. "You ain't going anywhere but jail, Richie Rich."

I backed up to the window. I'd never seen so much hatred and bile in someone's expression, and I couldn't help but think that the idea of Nakita taking this guy's life before he sullied his soul so far that he wouldn't even ask for forgiveness wasn't such a bad idea. I was thinking like a dark reaper, and I didn't like it.

Shoe was white-faced with anger. "You were with me when I wrote it. I'll tell them—"

"Tell them what?" Ace interrupted. "*You* trashed the school's files. The disc I left in the hospital is the same program. It's got your name on it, dude."

Standing before Ace, Shoe started to shake. "You are an ass," he said, and I gasped when he punched Ace. Right in the face.

"Shoe!" I shouted, but Ace was down, having hit the bed and slipped to the floor. Standing above him, Shoe shook his hand, swearing.

"You hit me!" Ace exclaimed, propped up on an elbow as he felt his mouth. "I'm freaking bleeding!"

"Yeah, and I'll hit you again unless you come with me to the police and tell them what you did. I wanted to trash the school's computer system, not hurt people!"

I already knew a trip to the police wasn't going to happen,

and I pulled Shoe back when Ace got to his feet, spitting blood on Shoe's carpet. "You're going to rot. Who are the police going to believe? It's all on your computer."

Shaking, I said in frustration, "I don't think I can stop Nakita from killing you, and you know what, Ace? I'm not even a bit sorry." I was, though. I ached for him to make a better choice. I knew he wouldn't. Maybe Nakita was right. The seraphs targeted only people who refused to see the light, even if you taped their eyes open and stood them in the sun.

The almost-sound of spilling broken glass slid through my awareness, and a softball-size haze of light darted into the room from the open window.

"Grace!" I exclaimed, and Shoe looked at me as if I were nuts. Either something had gone really right with Barnabas and Nakita, or it had gone really wrong.

The globe circled Ace as if getting a scent, then went to perch on Shoe's monitor. "Grace?" I questioned, suddenly unsure.

"Guardian angel two-T-four-five taking on a new charge, you lamebrain, dark-winged dark reaper," the light said snidely. "You lose."

My mouth dropped open, and I turned to the window when I realized what had happened. "No!" I cried, and my anger peaked when I saw Paul, smug and satisfied, standing in the bushes, his head level with the window.

"You idiot!" I exclaimed, and both Shoe and Ace turned to the window to see him. Damn it, this was my own fault. He must have been at the school, then followed us, waiting until I gave away who the mark was before assigning an angel to Ace.

"Done and done," Paul said snarkily. "You lose, Madison. I saved this one."

"Saved him for what?" I asked. Angrier than I'd ever been, I lunged to the window, grabbing his tunic and dragging him in.

"Ow! Hey!" Paul exclaimed, hitting the floor in a graceless pile. From the ceiling, the guardian angel was shouting, but no one but me could probably hear it. Shoe and Ace had drawn back, and I stood over Paul, wanting to give him a good kick.

"You stupid idiot!" I said, pissed. "I told you I was taking care of this! And you come in and muck it up! Why don't you find out the entire story before you start making *choices* for people! Thanks a hell of a lot, Paul!"

From outside in the hall, I heard Shoe's mom call out, "Honey? Is everything all right?"

Oh, crap!

We froze. Paul got up off the floor, his eyes wide. Ace was standing with his head craned back as his nose bled.

"We're fine, Mom," he called out with just the right amount of irritation, flexing his hand, which was now swollen from having hit Ace.

"Swell, swell, we're all good here," the angel chimed out.

"You guys want a snack or anything?" his mother asked, clearly concerned.

My estimation of Shoe's mom went higher. She hadn't burst in even when things were clearly not right. She was a cool lady for letting us work this out ourselves.

"No, Mom! We're fine!"

Fine, fine. We're all just spiffy keen.

No one spoke as her heels clicked away. Finally the guardian angel sighed, and Shoe put his back to his door, clearly frustrated. "Okay," he said, looking at Paul. "This is my room, and I want to know who you are and what's going on."

I couldn't tell him everything, but I stood in front of the window and crossed my arms over my middle. "This idiot just gave Ace a guardian angel!" I said, furious.

"Saved your scrawny butt," the guardian angel said, and I gave it a dark look. It sounded different from Grace, but I doubted that I'd be able to name it and break the hold Ron had put on it. Not a second time.

Ace brought his head down and sniffed back his bloody nose. "I got a guardian angel?"

"Him?" Shoe yelled. "He just framed me for crashing the hospital computers tomorrow."

"Yeah, I know. Ironic, isn't it?" I said, uncrossing my arms and turning to Ace. "You can't see her, but you just got a blessing from heaven—idiot. Nothing will touch you now until your scheduled death." Turning to Paul, I couldn't help myself and shouted, "Thanks a lot!"

This just wasn't my day. Here I was supposed to be impressing the seraphs that dark and light reapers could work together to save the lost, and I had failed spectacularly. At least Barnabas could make everyone forget the last twenty-four hours. If he was okay, that was. The guardian angel buzzed me, and I wasn't surprised as her wings came to a halt with the soft sound of sliding glass.

"You're not a dark reaper," she said. "You're the dark *time-keeper*! You're Madison? I heard about you! You gave Grace a name!"

I nodded, not wanting to say anything aloud and make Shoe or Ace any more aware of what was going on than they already were. Barnabas was a reaper, not a miracle worker.

"Just as well," the chiming ball of light said. "She wasn't very good at it."

A soft sound of affront slipped from me, and I stared at her.

Paul had gotten to his feet, and he stood next to Ace as if not quite knowing what to do. "You wanted him dead," he said, but he sounded unsure. "Ron was right."

I began to pace between the desk and the open window. "Ron is a shortsighted idiot," I muttered. Spinning, I pointed to Ace, now smiling as he dabbed at his nose with the hem of his shirt. "Do you know what that fine piece of work does now that you've given him a get-out-of-death-free card? He's going to go on and do it again, deluded and thinking it's a kick. He thinks it's his only way to make a mark on the world. He's dead, Paul," I said. "You may have saved his life, but his life is worthless. I had a chance to get him to change, but now he never will."

Edging away from Ace, Paul said, "You don't know that."

I arched my eyebrows at him. "I do. *I saw it.* Congratulations. You did real well on your scythe prevention. Saved him and everything." What was the difference between this scythe and my last one, where I had saved Susan on the boat, the first time I'd met Nakita? I'd changed her future with nothing more than showing her a near-death, and it hadn't even been hers. She had been marked because she was going to live her life distorting the truth to ruin people's lives just for the sensationalism. Seeing the reality of how precious life was and the tragedy of it being cut short had shown her what really mattered, and she had changed. But Ace . . . he knew his actions were going to end lives—and he didn't care. Except for what he could gain from it.

Ace was laughing, pulling out more tissue from the box by the bed. Making a happy sigh, he fell back onto the pillows. "I've got a guardian angel? Cool!" he said to the ceiling.

His guardian angel didn't seem very happy, if the gray blob on the mirror was any indication. I was pacing again; I couldn't help it. I was not going to let things end like this.

Paul was edging to the window, and Shoe was trying to wipe his fingerprints off the hospital entrance card. "You were going to end his life," Paul said slowly, and I glanced at Ace.

"I was trying to save it. But why, I don't have a clue."

Shoe had turned his back on us, and his fingers clicked over the keys. Rummaging for a blank disc, he slid it into the burner and clicked a button. "I'm not taking the blame for the hospital," he said emphatically.

Ace laughed from the bed. "You can't stop me. I just got me a guardian angel."

From the mirror, the ball of light sighed.

My temper was cooling. Shoe was probably burning a patch. Clearly he was having the same thoughts I was, since the hospital entrance card was now shoved into his back pocket. We could break in and upload the patch. There was just the lingering problem of Ace. The moment we left, Ace would call someone.

I turned to Paul, the beginnings of a plan in me. "You guys never stick around to find out what the people you save do after you bless them, do you?" I said sourly. What was done was done. *Fate,* I thought, wondering if I was wrong about choice being stronger than seraph vision. Paul was still looking at me, and I snapped, "Just leave, okay? You did your thing. I've got work to do."

Paul's expression became worried, and he looked at Ace. "What are you going to do?" he asked. "He's got a guardian angel."

"The people at the hospital don't," I said. "And you call me a murderer? Open your eyes!" I turned to Shoe, glad to see a determined slant to his expression as he popped the disc out of his computer and glared at Ace. "Is that the patch?" I asked, and he nodded. From the bed, Ace sat up.

"What are you doing?"

Shoe handed it to me, saying, "She's going to put the patch in for me while you and I sit here and play some WoW. If you want to call the cops, go ahead, but I'll break your fingers if you try it before that patch is in place. I'm not going down with lives on my conscience."

"You wouldn't," Ace said, wiping his nose. Blood smeared his face and his fingers, bits of tissue sticking to them.

Smiling grimly, I pushed Paul aside as I moved to the window. "You're a good person, Shoe. I'll do what I can." How was I going to do this? I didn't know a thing about computers.

Ace threw his tissues away. "You think Shoe can keep me here?" he said, moving to sit in Shoe's chair as if it were a throne and twisting it back and forth. "I got a guardian angel. Once that freak of a girl leaves, I'll have your mom in here. Then I'm calling *my* mom. I'm telling her you hit me and stole her entry card."

My jaw clenched, and Shoe, waiting by the door, frowned. I glanced at the guardian angel sitting on the edge of the mirror, and she made a little chirp of a sigh. "Damn it," I muttered. Maybe if I knew how my amulet worked, I could stay and Shoe could go, but I didn't.

Shifting nervously, Shoe said, "I didn't know angels could swear."

Paul made a face, looking as if he were eating something

sour. "She's not an angel."

"I'm just dead," I said. Frustrated, I looked at Paul. He met my gaze, his expression holding a hint—the barest whisper—of guilt. Barnabas and Nakita were nowhere to be seen. I so needed some help. I just needed to know how to use my amulet.

Use my amulet . . .

"Will, ah, you do me a favor?" I suddenly asked Paul, and it was hard to decide who was more surprised, the guardian angel, now a bright silver, or Paul, staring at me.

"Excuse me?"

I glanced at Ace, then back to him. "Will you just . . . watch him for a while?" I asked. "So Shoe and I can fix what we can?"

A curious look came into Paul's eyes. "I don't understand you, Madison."

Hope zinged through me. That hadn't been a no. The guardian angel clearly thought it was a great idea, darting about the ceiling as if she were a pixie high on a double espresso. "My dad doesn't understand me, either," I said, smiling. "Will you do it? Try to make up for screwing this up?"

"I didn't screw it up. I saved his life!" he said hotly, then looked at Ace staring at us with a murderous look. "Yeah. I'll do it," he added. "But you owe me."

"You think you're tougher than me?" Ace said as he stood up, and I tensed.

Paul reached for his amulet, and I shivered as something

went through me when he touched the divine. The guardian angel let out a yelp when Ace collapsed. Damn, that had been fast. "Wow," I whispered, totally impressed.

Shoe nudged Ace in the ribs with his foot. "I'm glad I'm on your side," he said, then pulled Ace's truck keys from his former friend's belt. "They have a camera on the hospital gate," he said in explanation as he edged past Paul and toward the window. "I don't want my car seen there."

He slipped out the window, leaning in as he said, "Cover for me if my mom knocks, okay?"

Paul nodded, looking both scared and excited.

"Can you change memories yet?" I asked him, aware of Shoe outside the window, but I really wanted to know.

"No," Paul admitted, looking almost chagrined, as though he'd tried and failed.

"Me neither," I said, feeling a surge of kinship. Smiling, I sat on the sill and swung my sneakers outside. It was cooler, and I shivered. Maybe I'd failed to save Ace's soul, but I could save the lives of some innocents. "Thanks, Paul. You're not so bad."

I dropped to the earth, and Shoe started across the dark grass, head down as he fumbled with Ace's keys.

"Madison!"

It was Paul, and I turned. He was in the window, the guardian angel on his shoulder. "You flashed forward?" he asked, looking uncertain. "Saw what comes of this?"

I nodded, wincing when Ace's music blared as Shoe started

his truck. "I saw what might be," I admitted, shivering at the memory. "He wasn't a bit sorry about it. I think what we're doing changes things, though." Paul said nothing, and, jiggling on my feet, I blurted, "I gotta go."

"Good luck!" he whispered loudly.

Smiling, I turned to run to Ace's truck. "Don't let Ron hear you say that," I muttered.

It was with a much lighter heart that I scrambled into the front passenger side of Ace's truck and buckled myself in. There were a thousand things that could go wrong, and someone was going to get in trouble even if everything went right, but Paul believed me.

And I was surprised to realize that meant a lot.

Eleven

Shoe put Ace's truck into park, but he didn't make one move to get out. Together we stared through the dirty windshield at the brightly lit emergency entrance. It looked quiet, but people were moving around inside.

"Scared?" I asked, feeling the memory of my heart echo in my thoughts. I hated it when it did that, and I forced it to stop.

His hand dropped from the steering wheel, and he looked across at me. "I've never broken into anything but the school, and you saw how well that went. Jeez, Madison, I've never even shoplifted."

"But you sat in your room and created a virus that can kill people by shutting down a hospital computer system?" I said with a huff.

"I did not create a program to kill people," he said hotly. "I made a virus to shut down the school for a day. That's it. Ace is a toad's ass."

It wasn't like I could argue with him. Head bobbing, I focused on the twin glass doors spilling light into the otherwise dimly lit parking lot. It suddenly occurred to me that I was running around with my amulet's resonance blaring since I'd left Nakita's and Barnabas's shielding. Puppy presents, this could come crashing down really fast. As soon as Ron wasn't occupied, he'd get curious.

Shoe rubbed his chin, clearly nervous. I knew the feeling. I was really worried about Barnabas, Nakita, and Grace. What if they got hurt? They were more powerful than I, but I was responsible for them. How did that happen?

"They aren't going to just let us walk in and sit down at a terminal," Shoe said with a sigh.

If Barnabas or Nakita were hurt, would Ron track me down to gloat? I was on borrowed time, and here I was sitting in a truck that didn't belong to either of us.

"How are we going to even get in there?" Shoe said, more loudly this time, since I hadn't answered him.

Nervous, I brought one of my knees to my chest to retie my sneaker. "It's too late to pretend to be visiting someone," I said. "How good an actor are you?"

Shoe's eyes widened in the faint security light. "You want to sneak in as an orderly?"

"No, but if you pulled into the emergency lot fast with me unconscious . . ."

Brow furrowing, he winced. "You think that will work?"

Remembering racing into the emergency room with Josh out cold and dying after being scythed by Nakita, I nodded. "I know it will. With all the distraction, you could easily slip into the back, with no one the wiser." *As long as I can keep my fake heartbeat going.* "Eventually they'll stabilize me and leave. It might take hours. Unless . . ."

Shoe gazed at me, waiting. "Unless what?"

"Uh, unless I play dead. They'll put me in the morgue pretty quick."

"Yeah, like that will work," he said around a snort.

I grabbed his hand and held it to my wrist. "I told you, I'm dead. See? No pulse. Unless I work at it, that is."

My heart gave one thump at the feel of his fingers around my wrist, and then it was silent.

Shoe's expression shifted from annoyance, to wonder, to fear. Pulling his hand from me, he got a sick look on his face. "It's a trick or something," he said.

Here I am again, sitting in a truck, trying to convince another guy that I'm dead, I thought. It sounded like a country song gone bad. My death was so messed up. Sighing, I said, "Good. Don't believe it. Just go along with it for a few more hours. You've got the patch?"

He touched his pocket and nodded.

"They're going to want to know who I am," I said, taking my wallet out of my pocket and putting it in the glove box, having to wedge aside another handful of music discs. My phone went next to it, and I hesitated. It was my only link to my dad. Putting it aside felt wrong.

"I so don't want my dad getting a call that I'm in a morgue half a state away," I said. "Can you tell them my name is Wendy?" Wendy wouldn't mind. She'd think it was hilarious. "Tell them you met me at the mall and we were going to a movie or something, and I just fell over?"

Shoe didn't look good. Actually, he was almost green in the dim security lights. "I don't know . . ." he started.

"Oh, for God's sake!" I exclaimed, feeling the pinch of time. "You're going to be blamed for three deaths, and you're worried about lying to the receptionist about where we met? Take me in, and when they tell you I've died, get upset and ask if you can go to the bathroom to throw up. Meet me at the elevators at the lowest floor. You've got an access key."

He touched his pocket where Ace's mother's ID was, and, looking pained, he nodded. "Why don't you just take the patch and upload it?" he asked as he brought it out.

The sight of the dripping black wing shivered through me. "Me?" I said. "I don't know anything about computers. You have to do it."

Reluctantly he slid it away. "What about after?" he asked. "You dead? Me bringing you in? The cops?" Then he paused.

"You said Barnabas could change memories."

I nodded, and, looking even more uncomfortable, Shoe licked his lips. "Don't change mine, okay?" he asked. "I want to remember this."

"Okay," I said quickly, just wanting to get on with it. I didn't know how long they would let me lie there before moving me downstairs. "When this is over, I can always simply go back to the morgue and get off the table," I said. "They'll think their instruments were off and I wasn't really dead. It's a freaking miracle."

"I mean it," Shoe said, his voice loud, and I looked at him. "Don't make me forget. If you take that from me . . . what's the point?"

My heart gave a thump and stilled. "Okay," I said, meaning it this time.

He looked at me for a long moment, then put the truck back into drive. "This had better work," he muttered.

"It'll work," I said, but it was kind of scary. I'd have to make sure my heart didn't start up, and it usually did when I was stressed. And I'd have to make sure I didn't smile and ruin it. If they put me in a drawer, I was going to be stuck until Shoe found me. But there weren't many choices here. If the patch wasn't in place by six, people were going to die. It would be my fault.

Nervous, I slumped in the seat against the door and concentrated on listening to the emptiness of no heartbeat. Slowly it settled and stopped. Identity hidden—check. Pulse stopped—check. *My amulet,* I thought, worried that someone might try to take it off me.

"Wait!" I said loudly, and the truck jerked to a stop. "I have to hide my amulet," I said sheepishly.

Shoe's eyebrows went up in question, and I settled myself to concentrate, glad that I'd been working on this. Taking my amulet in my hand, I thought about it, how it felt in my grip, smooth, warm, and how it was a violet so deep that it was really black. I looked at it with my mind's eye, seeing how it touched the divine, filtered it so I wouldn't destroy myself when time echoed in my thoughts. It resonated with the sound of my soul, of the universe. It felt alive. And if I twisted the weight of it just so . . . light would bend around it.

A warm sensation filled me. Knowing it had worked, I opened my eyes and let go of my amulet. It thumped back against me, but it was gone. Damn, I loved it when I could do something.

"Oh, my God, it went invisible," Shoe said, sounding scared. "Shit. You really are dead," he said, white-faced.

I smiled, trying to reassure him. "Now you look like you've got a dead girl in your truck. Let's go."

Taking a deep breath, he turned to the hospital entrance. "I'm going to get in so much trouble for this," he whispered, hands shaking as he put the truck in drive and revved the engine.

I closed my eyes again, forcing myself to go limp. I'd made

my amulet invisible before, but never when it mattered like it did now. I'd have three balls in the air, and I didn't know if I could do it. I had to keep the memory of my heart quiet, keep myself from twitching when they tried to bring me to life, and I had to keep my amulet hidden. I didn't know if I could do this.

But I had to.

The double doors shut with a hush of sound when the orderly who had wheeled me down to the morgue went to get a soda. In an explosion of motion, I sat up, shoving the sheet off me as if it were a snake. Angry, I looked down at my shirt, trying to get the ragged edges to cover me. It was my favorite shirt, the one I'd bought for the first day of school, and they ripped it as if it were a discount special. My tights, too, had suffered, but my shirt was the worst where they had poked, prodded, and arced electricity through me.

"Son of a puppy," I muttered as I swung my feet over the edge and let them dangle. There were new holes in my arms, too, and I pulled out the needles they had left in me and tossed them on the gurney. No less than four lab techs had tried to get blood from me, failing because there was none to get. I was never going to play dead again. *Never!*

Holding my torn shirt closed, I slid from the table. My bare feet slapped the cold tile, and, looking down, I swore again. For crying out loud—I had a toe tag. When had they put *that* on?

"Where are my shoes?" I muttered, looking under the gurney to find nothing there. Fortunately, my amulet was still around my neck. If they had tried to take that, I would have flipped. It was visible now. I'd quit hiding it the moment the sheet had been pulled over me. When they had given up on me . . . It hadn't been a nice feeling at all.

Mood sour, I strode across the dimly lit room, snatching a lab coat from a coathook behind the desk. I shoved my arms in and buttoned it up to cover my torn shirt and my ripped tights. My heart had given a blip once while I'd been on the table, and they'd gone all out trying to get it started again. I'd never felt so violated, but at least they hadn't cut off my bra.

"Hey, those are mine!" I said when I found my earrings on the orderly's desk. Mad, I shoved one, then the other into my ears. Still barefoot, I headed for the double doors. I had to find Shoe. Angry at the world, I pushed the doors open and looked out. The hall was empty. One of the fluorescent lights was out, and farther down the low-ceilinged corridor, another flickered. It smelled like bleach. The other direction appeared about the same, but at the end of it was a set of silver elevator doors. I was so out of there.

The toe tag rasped on the tile, and, not slowing, I leaned

down, yanked it off, and let it hit the floor. I hadn't been "dead" very long, and I was betting Shoe was still upstairs.

From behind me came a masculine voice calling, "Ma'am? You dropped something."

My teeth clenched, and I spun around, eyes narrowing when I found it was the orderly who had wheeled me down here to the mangled tune of "Satisfaction." The same one who had swiped my earrings, I'd bet. "What!" I snapped, very conscious of my bare feet and my purple-tinted hair. Not to mention my ripped shirt and tattered tights. Posing as a doctor was out, but maybe I could be a lab tech having a bad day.

The guy's pudgy face became surprised. "Uh, sorry," he said as he came forward, slower now. "I thought you were a doctor." Stopping, he looked at the morgue tag, then at me, then at the doors to his right. The bottle of pop in his hand started to slip. "Ah . . ."

Angry, I strode back, my bare feet slapping. "Thanks," I said, snatching the toe tag and jamming it into the lab coat pocket. Giving him a last glare, I turned and started back to the end of the hall to the elevator. Behind me, there was a nervous shifting of shoes.

"Hey, uh, weren't you . . ." the guy said, then hesitated, thinking. I got three steps farther down the hall, and he shouted, "Hey!"

I didn't turn around, but every muscle in me tensed as I smacked the up button. Almost instantly the doors slid apart, but I jerked to a halt when Shoe looked out at me, shocked. His eyes went behind me, and I wasn't surprised when I heard the orderly shout, "Hey, you! Wait up!"

Shoe's eyes were huge as he took in my lab coat and angry expression, and he rocked back, saying, "Uh, you okay?"

"Find me a broom closet, will you?" I muttered, and he darted out of the elevator.

I stiffened as the orderly came up behind me, huffing and puffing. I'd had enough. The stuff they did to dead people sucked. The last thing I wanted to do was answer this guy's questions as to why I was up and walking.

"You got a problem?" I exclaimed as I turned to him. It had the desired effect, and he stopped short. Behind him, Shoe had found a tiny room with a wheeled bucket and mop. Jabbing my finger at the guy, I forced him to take a step backward.

"You're alive . . ." the orderly stammered, his eyes going to my earrings, back where they belonged—in my ears.

"Not really, but you're a thief," I said tightly. "Take a time-out," I added, shoving him back into the closet.

Arms pinwheeling, the guy fell back. Tripping on the bucket, he went down, staring up at me when I reached in and grabbed his keys off his belt. I rocked back out of the way, and Shoe yanked the door shut, almost catching the guy's white sneaker.

"I'd guess that one," Shoe said as he pointed out a key with MAINTENANCE on it, and I jammed it into the lock and gave it a twist.

"Hey!" came faintly from the closet, and I exhaled, feeling vastly better.

Shoe eyed the closet, laughing. "Make a new friend?" he asked, and I jumped when the orderly rattled the handle and pounded on the door.

Embarrassed, I felt my anger fizzle. "He stole my earrings," I said, glad I hadn't found them in his earlobes. Skulls and cross-bones were harder to find than one might expect.

"Let me out!" came from the closet.

"Thanks," I said to Shoe as we turned back to the elevator and I hit the up button.

"For what?"

Suddenly shy, I looked at Shoe, his hands in his pockets and his shirt casually untucked. "For coming to find me," I said.

The elevator wasn't back yet, and he glanced askance at me. "I wanted to make sure you were okay. I mean, you were dead."

"I still am."

He became even more nervous, shifting from foot to foot as he watched for the up light to glow. "Yeah," he admitted, "but . . . you're okay, too."

I smiled, reaching out to mock punch his shoulder. "It's just my body that's dead."

Shoe took a deep breath, exhaling loudly. "Ah, we need a quiet computer."

From the closet came a soft, "Damn, no bars."

"There's a computer in the morgue," I suggested, and Shoe looked down the empty hallway, his eyebrows high in speculation. I knew exactly what he was thinking: Why go somewhere else when the only person down here was locked in a closet?

"Sounds good to me," Shoe said, and we started for the double doors, his shoes squeaking on the tile and my bare feet silent. "If the virus is on the computer, then I can connect to the server from here and upload the patch."

My smile went wider. This was going to work. Finally, something was going my way.

"Guys?" the orderly called, starting to sound frantic. "Anyone? Hello?"

Shoe looked down as we entered the morgue. "Why did they take your shoes off?" he asked, and I suddenly became very conscious of my torn shirt, hidden under the coat.

"They have to put the toe tag somewhere," I said, slowing to a stop and wondering if my shoes might be in one of the lockers against the wall. I wasn't a connoisseur of morgues, but this one was nicer than the one I'd woken up dead in the first time. There was only the gurney I'd come in on, and I guessed this was a holding area where they kept the bodies before they were given . . . permanent shelving. That was probably in the room beyond the doors with BIOHAZARD stenciled on them. I wasn't going to go look. I was just glad they dropped me off and left before putting me in a cold drawer. I hadn't been looking forward to having to knock to be let out.

"This guy is a slob," Shoe said as he headed for the scratched desk. With a single finger, he shoved the remains of the guy's chicken dinner across the faded fake-wood desktop and sat in the rolling chair. "Look, he's got grease all over the keyboard," Shoe said, disgusted.

I picked up my file. JANE DOE. Yup, that was me. CAUSE OF DEATH, UNDETERMINED. Yuck, I'd been down for an autopsy. I started feeding the contents, sheet by sheet, into a paper shredder, feeling better as my record disappeared. "Can you imagine eating down here?" I said between sheets. "That is just gross." *Kind of like waking up barefoot in the morgue.*

With a flourish, Shoe took control of the computer, pulling the chair up close and typing an address into the window to bring up a serious-looking black screen. Watching his proficiency, I mentally kicked myself for not knowing that it hadn't been him in my first flash forward. Shoe was really good at this. *Exceptionally good,* I hoped as I finished destroying my file and came to stand behind him so I could watch him work.

"Let's see what we've got . . ." he said softly, oblivious to where he was as he found the familiar in a new setting. He tapped a few more keys, and a search began. "Yup," he said when something immediately popped up: a little black bird icon next to the string of nonsense letters and numbers that meant nothing to me. Black bird. Like the dripping artwork Ace had made his trademark. I hadn't seen a real black wing in two days, but they seemed to be everywhere.

"There it is," he said, glancing back at me with victory in his eyes. "We can do this from here. I just need to do some backtracking to make sure that it's a two-way communication, then drop the patch in."

He was excited. My heart gave a thump, and I smiled. "How long will that take?" I asked as I pushed the greasy chicken into the trash and sat on the desk. The orderly was really close to the elevator. If he kept shouting, someone would eventually hear him.

Shoe shrugged, totally unruffled and cool. "Few minutes."

Relief spilled into me, and I exhaled a breath I'd probably taken five minutes ago. "That's great," I said, beaming. "Shoe, you're fantastic. I wouldn't know the first thing to do."

"Yeah, well, it's what I do," he said awkwardly, but then he blinked at me. "What happened to your shirt?"

My hands flew to the lab coat to make sure I was covered. I was, but I slid from the desk, holding the lab coat tighter about my middle. "Uh, I was dead," I said, flustered. "They tore it while trying to get my heart beating."

"Sorry," he said, seeming to mean it. Turning back to the keyboard, he started tapping.

"It was my favorite shirt, too," I said, wondering how I was going to keep this and my tights from my dad. Oh, swell, my dad. Crap, I'd promised to call my mother, too.

The sound of the elevator dinging in the distance brought both Shoe's and my heads up. This wasn't good. Maybe they'd found someone else to try sticking me for blood. "Just do your thing," I said as I headed for the door. "No matter what, don't stop. I'll keep whoever it is out."

But as my hand was reaching to push the left side of the door open, Nakita blew in through the right. Shocked, I stumbled back.

She was in white again, the designer jeans and red top I'd given her replaced by white slacks and a clingy white shirt that made her one smooth line. Her amulet blazed a deep violet against her skin, and her sword was in her hand. Tiny white boots edged in gold were spread wide on the bleach-faded tile. It was what she had worn the afternoon she'd tried to kill me. Obviously something was wrong.

"Nakita!" I exclaimed, then shivered when something slid over my aura to hide it.

At the computer, Shoe blew his breath out and started to type again.

"I trusted you!" Nakita exclaimed, her eyes dark as she stood before me, shaking.

Bewildered, I stared until I remembered. *Ace.* He'd gotten a guardian angel. *Crap.* "Paul followed us from the school," I blurted, dropping back as she came forward step by stiff step. "I didn't know he was there! By the time I knew what he was doing, it was too late. Nakita, I didn't tell him it was Ace. He followed me!" I almost shouted, yelping when my butt hit the rolling gurney behind me. Remembering her killing my predecessor before my very eyes, I let my gaze drop to her amulet. It was as if it were throwing black shards of light into the shadows of the room. Nakita had paused, listening, but her grip on her sword was still white-knuckled. I think she wanted to believe me but was afraid.

"The seraphs were right," I pleaded. "Talking to Ace wouldn't have made any difference. But Shoe can still save the people Ace was going to kill."

Nakita lowered her sword an inch. Her cheeks were spotted with red, and I gripped the rolling table behind me with both hands.

"I don't *care* about the people who are going to die," she said, making Shoe pause in his typing. "Saving them is *not my job*! Their souls are beautiful and the seraphs will rejoice. It's wounded souls that concern me. I care for the wounded, Madison, not the well."

My mouth dropped open in a silent "oh" of understanding. She was a dark reaper. She *killed people* to save their souls. She thought what I was trying to do was foolish. And yet she stood there, shielding my soul from Ron's detection as she tried to understand.

"Taking Ace's soul before he sullied it beyond redemption was my task," she said, and I couldn't tell what she was feeling. "His soul depended upon me, and I failed him utterly because

I trusted you. You made a deal with the light timekeeper's acolyte. You let him give Ace a guardian angel so I wouldn't be able to kill his body. Admit it!"

Shoe was staring. His fingers were still, and the silence soaked into me. "Keep working, Shoe," I said, not looking away from Nakita. "I didn't give him Ace," I said to her, and she grew more agitated, a confused angel with a sword. "Paul gave Ace his guardian angel before I even knew he was there. You didn't fail him. I did. I'm sorry, but I didn't betray you! Not on purpose."

Nakita fingered her amulet, confusion pinching her eyes. Because of me, black wings had eaten her memories. Not all of them, but enough so that she had felt the touch of death. The sound of her screams as she realized there was such a thing as an end had been awful. She alone among the angels knew what it was to fear death. She alone knew the bitterness of loss. And I still couldn't get her to understand why I wanted to end the early scythings.

"I went to Shoe's room. I talked to Ace," she said. "He told me you made a deal with the rising light timekeeper. He laughed at me. You lied! Just like Kairos!"

"I didn't lie," I said quickly, reaching to touch her, only to drop my hand. "I forgot about Paul, and because of that, Ace got an angel. I am so, so sorry, Nakita. It was my mistake. I did make a deal with Paul, but it was for him to keep Ace from interfering while Shoe patched the virus. I was so mad at Paul,

I could have scythed him myself. But my goal was never to keep Ace from getting an angel. I was trying to show him what his choices were going to bring about and hopefully get him to change so his life would have meaning. I can still do that. I know it goes against your nature, but I thought you understood. Or at least were trying to understand. I thought you were helping me."

Her anger hesitated, and, looking confused, she lowered her gaze. "Ace won't change," she said. "You said it yourself. And now his soul is truly lost."

Taking a step forward, I touched her shoulder, pulling back when her head came up. There were tears in her eyes, and she wiped them, looking shocked to be crying.

"It's not over yet." *How am I going to change a millennia of beliefs if I can't even convince one reaper who wants to understand but can't?* "I can fix this," I said, and she stared at me as if wondering why I was bothering. "If we don't do something, Shoe will take the blame for Ace's choices. But if Ace has to face the fallout, he might change his own fate."

Fate, I thought, tasting it in my mind as it dissolved on my tongue. I hated that word, but it had piqued Nakita's interest. She knew fate.

"You think?" she asked, her shoulders easing as hope softened the lines of anger in her face.

"I hope," I said, wanting to be perfectly clear.

Nakita frowned at Shoe, as if seeing him for the first time, his typing starting and stopping as he muttered to the computer. Change was hard for her, but she'd try for me, her timekeeper, the one who'd damaged her perfect belief. Her sword disappeared. "Then I probably shouldn't have hit Paul," she said, biting her lower lip innocently. Her eyes landed on my bare feet, and she blinked. "Where are your shoes?"

The worst of it seemed to be over, and I eased away from the gurney. "I don't know. Are Barnabas and Grace okay?" I asked.

Nakita was scanning the morgue, clearly not concerned. "They're coming," she said as she went to the bank of lockers, running her fingers over them as if searching for something. "After you left, Ron talked to Paul through his amulet. As soon as he found out that Ace got his guardian angel, Ron laughed, said unkind things, and left. Grace and Barnabas followed him to be sure he wasn't going to find you, seeing as your aura was chiming all over heaven and earth. I went to Shoe's house to see for myself. Then I came here."

Nakita twisted and yanked on a locker handle, and it popped open, the hinges bent. "I'm sorry," she said as she reached in and came out with my shoes and socks. "I should have trusted you. I don't understand what you are trying to do. Maybe if I understood why."

Her steps silent, she crossed the room to hand me my yellow sneakers. "It's okay," I said as I accepted them. "I don't know what I'm doing half the time, either. I just do what feels right."

Nakita smiled faintly. "I probably shouldn't have knocked Paul out—even if it felt right, too. His amulet is powerful, but it's not a timekeeper's."

She didn't just hit him, but knocked him out? Leaning against the gurney, I looked up from putting my socks on, hopping on one foot when the gurney started to roll. "Nakita . . . please tell me you're kidding. He was there to keep Ace from leaving."

Wincing, Nakita took a breath to answer, but she stopped, spinning to the hall when the twin doors crashed open. It was Ace, and he wasn't happy.

Jeez, can this get any worse? "Ace!" I shouted, almost panicking, one sock on, the other dangling from a finger.

"Get away from the computer, Shoe," he demanded, his black shirt hiding the blood that dripped from his nose, but I could smell it like a warning, almost see a red glow flaring from him. *Is it his aura? Am I finally starting to see auras?*

"Like I said, I probably shouldn't have hit Paul," Nakita admitted.

Shoe didn't look up, his fingers typing furiously. "Go to hell," he muttered, trusting us to keep Ace off him. "I'm not taking the blame for this."

Ace predictably went for Shoe, and Nakita lunged forward. "Back . . ." she threatened, but her motion to pull her sword faltered when a glowing ball of light hummed in after him. It was his guardian angel, and I knew from experience that they worked by making things go wrong. The more Nakita tried to hurt him, the worse it would become. The angel might not believe in saving Ace, but she'd do it.

"Keep working, Shoe!" I shouted, angling to get between them and raising my hands in placation when his guardian angel hummed a warning. All Ace saw was me looking as if I were begging for him to be a good little boy. *If only I could reason with this angel like I do Grace.*

Peeved, I glanced at Nakita as I settled into a martial arts stance, one sock on, one off. "You not only let him get away, you let him follow you?" I said to Nakita.

"Not exactly," she said, then stomped her foot at Ace to make him drop back a step. "Well, maybe," she added. "Ace woke up when I hit Paul. I knew he was following me, but I didn't think it mattered. Madison, I'm sorry. I thought we had failed!"

Ace began moving, and all three of us shifted to stay with him: me, Nakita, and the guardian angel. "Shoe, you're pathetic," Ace said, and I wondered why he was limping. "Girls guarding you? Get away from the computer or I'm going to pound you."

Yeah, like that was going to happen. "Don't stop, Shoe!" I encouraged. Ace took another step forward with his hands fisted, and Nakita drew her sword. I felt dizzy. Everything was spiraling out of control.

"You crazy chick!" Ace shouted, knowing he had a guardian angel, but not ready to trust it. "I'm not afraid of you!"

"Come closer," she encouraged, her hair falling about her face to make her look dangerous.

Shoe was clicking and clacking. Then he stopped, and as he whispered a hushed, "Yes!" I heard the whine of the CD tray slide open. *We're going to do it! We're actually going to do it!* I thought, elation filling me.

But Ace heard Shoe, too, and he gritted his teeth, a wild look coming over his face. And suddenly, as I stood between Ace and Shoe, I felt the strength drain from me.

A thin tracing of blue spun from the overhead lights to pool on the morgue's floor.

Not now!

Frightened, I dropped back, holding my stomach as if I could keep myself in. Nakita turned to me, and I panicked as the lights filled the entire room with a blue haze, spilling out from the fixtures in a flood. I was going to flash forward. Ace had made a decision, and his future was changing. This was not what I needed right now!

"Madison?" Nakita called, but her voice sounded tinny, as if from far away.

Dizzy, I looked at her. I could see her wings behind her, existing an instant in the future and therefore invisible to everyone except perhaps the guardian angel hovering over all of us. Her eyes were silver. Nakita was almost too beautiful to look at, and it took several tries for me to whisper, "I'm going to flash forward, Nakita. Don't let me go!"

Her blade drooped in her confusion, and, seeing an opening, Ace moved.

"No!" I shouted, but I collapsed as the world turned inside out. Nakita lunged for me, her hands catching me just before I hit the floor. Shoe was shouting, but my head was turned to the ceiling. And as the blueshift intensified, the ceiling, the walls, everything melted away . . . and the beauty of the stars slammed into me.

I gasped, the pain of so much beauty slicing through me like fire. The ringing of sounds never before heard exploded within my soul. Tears filled my eyes, and I shook in Nakita's arms.

"It hurts . . ." I moaned, and she turned my face to her. The terrible beauty of the heavens was replaced by the tragic beauty of an angel I had damaged—Nakita, to whom I had taught the meaning of fear. I had done it to her. Me. But the seraphs were right: The fear was a gift, and it made her more than she had been before, even as it tore at her.

"Close your eyes," Nakita whispered in a terrified hush, and I buried my face against her, sobbing. It was too much. I was mortal, and to see the divine was killing me. How did Ron do this?

The sound of fighting pulled at me, and I felt my awareness drift in the room as my illusion of a body started to go indistinct. And then . . . I was Ace, feeling his anger, his fear. His everything.

I hate you, I thought with him, unable to separate from him, and with a loud shout, he swung his fist at Shoe, who was rising up from his chair. I howled as his fist connected and the pain shot up his arm. Shaking the throbbing from our hand, I watched Ace's satisfaction as Shoe rocked back to the chair and fell off it, his hand on his jaw.

No! I screamed into Ace's mind as he hit the delete button and yanked the connection from the wall. I had no idea whether there'd been enough time to load it completely, and as I tried to take control of a future that hadn't happened yet, Ace picked up the keyboard and smashed it against Shoe's head when he tried to stand.

"Get up!" I heard Ace say, both in our shared ears and in our shared mind, furious. "I'm going to kill you!"

I wanted to throw up, but I was trapped, trying to change things but unable to even make myself heard. This was a freaking nightmare. And above it hovered Ace's guardian angel, weeping for him, weeping for me—a glittering silver cloud falling from her to turn the blue to silver until it touched Ace's aura and was repelled.

Shoe looked up from the floor. "Get a grip, Ace," he breathed, staggering as he rose to stand in front of it. "We're talking about real people. What the hell is wrong with you?"

"Wrong with me?" Ace shouted.

Ace, stop! I screamed, unheard, but as if in response, a heavier wash of blue filled my awareness. Vertigo made me clutch at anything, memories and visions slipping past me like a maelstrom.

I was going deeper into the future, and my mind rebelled. With a nauseating sensation, and sounding like a coin spinning to a stop, the blue around me shifted and spun until it settled to a steady solid blue.

I was still in the morgue, still in Ace. The police were here, and the guy I'd locked in the closet was standing by the lockers, looking bewildered. Shoe was sitting on the floor with his head down, cuffs on his wrists. And I was feeling pretty damn good even as I was aching in despair. I had to get out. I was trapped in Ace's head—feeling his satisfaction mixing with my pain was driving me insane.

"So when I found out what he was doing," I heard myself say, thinking I was damn clever for thinking up this plan, "I followed him from the school to the hospital. He snuck in, locked the guy in the closet, and put the virus in the morgue's computer. Isn't that sick? Trying to kill people from a morgue computer?"

The cops were nodding, and the one holding Shoe's shoulder gave him a disgusted look.

That's a lie! I thought, not feeling a twinge in Ace's conscience.

"I told him not to," Ace lied, and Shoe's jaw clenched as he refused to say anything. "It was just lucky that I had the patch. I put it in place, and then he hit me! Broke the keyboard over my head. He's crazy, I tell you. Nuts! He did the same thing at the school. He could have killed someone!"

The cops turned to the orderly. "Is that what happened?" they asked him, and the shaken man looked up blankly.

"I don't remember," he said, and I recognized his confused expression as one I'd seen on my dad's face too often. He remembered something, but logic said it was impossible. My reapers had come and gone, leaving broken lives in their wake.

He's lying! I shouted in Ace's mind, and the guardian angel in the corner looked up from her weeping. Then I hissed into Ace's thoughts, *You're a liar. A disgusting liar. I should have let Nakita scythe you.* This was so unfair. It looked like the patch had gone in, but somehow, by trying to set things right, I'd put Ace into the perfect place to do the most damage to Shoe's credibility and secure his own. Especially when no one seemed to remember my being here. Except perhaps the guardian angel.

I gathered myself to try to change a future that hadn't happened yet, but the blue tint overlaying everything seemed to hesitate. For an instant, everything went normal, colors, sounds, everything. In that second of clarity, Shoe looked at Ace, but I think he was seeing me, his expression bewildered and betrayed. And then . . . the world flashed red.

With a wrench hard enough to make me groan, I felt myself tear from the fabric of time. Gasping, I took a breath that was wholly mine. There was no thudding in my chest. No blood in my veins—and Nakita's grip on me was so tight it hurt.

"I'm back," I whispered, and her hands on me jerked.

"Madison!" she exclaimed, and I looked up at her, seeing my fear reflected in her silvered eyes. But it was the memory of Shoe's haunted look that wouldn't leave my mind.

A crash pulled my attention from her, and I realized that everything had taken all of an instant. Shoe was getting up off the floor, dazed but determined, holding his jaw. I'd seen this before. Lived it.

"Get up!" Ace was screaming at him. "I'm going to kill you!"

"Madison?" Nakita said, helping me sit up. "Are you okay? I've never seen anyone flash forward."

"I'll be fine." Wobbling to my feet, I grasped for anything to steady me, latching onto the rolling gurney. Bad choice, and I stumbled until Nakita caught me. "It really takes a lot out of me." Crap, I could hardly stand up.

"Get a grip, Ace," Shoe breathed, staggering as he stood. "We're talking about real people. What the hell is wrong with you?"

"Wrong with me?" Ace shouted, and my eyes went to the angel above us, right where I remembered seeing her. She was crying as it all played out again. I knew she'd seen everything I had seen during the flash forward. She had bathed in the divine and could live the past and the future all at once. And she was chained by a will not her own, but Ron's.

Swallowing hard, I leaned heavily into Nakita. "You know what happens," I said to the angel, and the angel turned to me, surprised. "I never wanted to end his life, and I'm not going to do it now. Fate or choice. They can be the same. As the dark timekeeper, I ask you to do as you would—without breaking the constraints of your previous charge."

Ace had yanked the cord from the wall, and as Shoe tried to stop him from snapping the CD in half, Ace shoved him into the wall behind the desk, following it with a punch to Shoe's gut. Exhaling in a puff of pained air, Shoe slid out of sight behind the desk.

And though I couldn't see beyond the shimmering glow that surrounded the guardian angel, I knew she smiled at me, bathing me in the first feeling of peace I'd had since I stood on a Greek island on the other side of the world and agreed to try to change the world. "Is this the present?" she asked, adding a bewildered, "Sometimes I can't tell."

I nodded, and she darted closer, the glow of her seeming to warm my face. "I like you," she chimed, the words tingling across me in waves. "You use your love to see the world. It makes everything harder for you, but if it were easy, then everyone could do it."

I had no clue what she was talking about, but I watched her fly into the fray, shifting the phone cord up an inch. As if choreographed to music, Ace stepped back, tripping on it. Shouting in surprise, he went down.

It was all the break Shoe needed. Rising up from behind the desk, he flung his hair out of his eyes, blood from his cheek smearing his hands and face. With a furious yell, he launched himself at Ace, and the two of them slid across the tiled floor, Ace's head thumping into it. I felt the world hiccup as fate shifted, and I took a gulp of air, feeling like I needed it.

"This isn't a game, Ace!" Shoe shouted, oblivious to Nakita and me. "These are real people, with families and kids!"

"Why should I care?" Ace snarled, and Shoe hauled off and punched him twice, first in the gut to make Ace lose all his breath in one go, then across the jaw with his left. Ace made a tiny grunt of pain, then went still.

"Because you're hurting people to make yourself feel good," Shoe said, staggering up and going to the computer. Above them, the angel cheered, her tears bathing both Ace and Shoe. Something had changed. I just hoped it was for the better.

Leaning heavily on the desk, Shoe plugged the keyboard back in, hitting a few buttons before turning to me with a tired smile. "It's in there," he said, then louder, toward Ace, "It's in there, you sack of toad crap. I'm not taking the blame for this! Not by a long shot!"

Dazed, I stared at Shoe, wondering if it was truly a different future that we'd all be living, or if Ace was going to somehow twist this again.

God help me. Is this what my life is going to be like?

Ace's arm moved, angling under him as if he were going to get up. Nakita strode over to him and stepped on his back to make him flop back down with a groan. I looked up at his guardian angel, now glowing with a bright, hazy light.

"No one is trying to kill him," she chimed cheerfully, then darted to the ceiling when the morgue doors were shoved open and Barnabas came in. Grace was with him, and I watched in openmouthed awe when the two guardian angels dipped and bobbed in a weird display of greeting.

"Is it patched? What happened!" Barnabas asked, looking at Nakita, who was now sitting on Ace, checking her nail polish. Shoe was breathing hard, sitting in the rolling chair and dabbing at his cheek with a tissue.

Nakita shrugged, looking almost disappointed that we hadn't simply killed him. "Madison has to do things the hard way."

My sock was across the room, and, blowing my breath out, I went to get it, sitting down right there on the cold tile floor to put it on. Not a whisper of a heartbeat echoed in my thoughts, and after feeling Ace's, I missed it. Worse, though, I was tired. I felt unreal and thin, as if part of me were still lost somewhere between the now and the next.

"You flashed forward again," Barnabas said, coming close, only to draw to a confused stop at my feet. I'd gotten my sock on, and I made a grasping gesture toward my sneakers, still on the gurney.

"It was awful," Nakita admitted while Barnabas fetched my shoes. "It was like she wasn't there."

"I don't feel so good," I said, my hands shaking as I put first one, then the other sneaker on. Looking at the skulls and crossbones on the laces, I wondered if I could do this. A thousand years of being inside people, watching them ruin their lives. No wonder Kairos had simply sent his reapers to kill the marked. A tear formed and fell, and, miserable, I tied my skull-and-crossbones laces in careful, perfect loops. I thought we had changed fate, but it was hard. Really hard.

"You failed?" Barnabas whispered as I wiped at my eye, and I shook my head.

"I think we succeeded," I said to make him even more confused.

"Are you okay, Madison?" Nakita asked. Barnabas reached to pull me up, and I couldn't do anything but try not to cry. I wasn't doing very well at that, either.

"I'm okay," I finally managed, wobbling on my feet and trying to imagine a lifetime of crap like this. "I'm just going to go crazy. That's all there is to it."

In a graceful motion, Nakita got up off of Ace. The idiot gathered himself to stand, but a pan of morgue tools somehow happened to slide off a nearby counter, beaning him. Groaning, he collapsed again while Grace and the other guardian angel gave each other what looked to be the angel equivalent of a high five. "He's still alive." Ace's guardian angel giggled, and I wondered if I was going to have to do something about this before Ace was accidented to death, but remembering Ace's hatred that had echoed in me, I decided I wouldn't worry about it.

"Is flashing forward supposed to be like that?" Nakita asked as she took my other elbow.

On my other side, I felt more than saw Barnabas shrug. "I don't know. Ron never said. How about Kairos? Did he ever look this tired to you?"

Nakita shook her head, her expression worried. Sighing, I leaned heavily on them. It was over, but there was still a lot to do. I'd gotten rid of my file, but there was probably something upstairs. And the guy in the closet. And Shoe . . .

"I'm really hungry," I said, the memory of being inside Ace making me feel ill. "Can we go get a burger?"

Nakita turned to me, her surprise mirrored by Barnabas's. Sighing, I sent my gaze to Shoe and Ace. "All of us?" I added. "I'm starving," I said, shocked to realize I was. "Besides," I said softly so Shoe couldn't hear, "we can take care of their memories there and leave them maybe as friends or something."

Instead of answering me, Barnabas looked over the morgue. "Is the patch in place?" he asked Shoe.

Shoe rolled his chair over to the computer. His expression was relieved, and he pocketed the disc. "Yes."

Barnabas straightened, gesturing for Nakita to get Ace. "Burgers sound good to me," he said with a startling amount of enthusiasm. We'd probably have no problem getting out of the hospital even with letting the guy out of the closet. Not with two reapers and two guardian angels.

Thoughts of salty fries and cold pop made my mouth water

as I followed Barnabas, Ace, and Shoe out into the empty hallway. I was tired and depressed . . . and hungry. This wasn't the ending I had expected. Had I won? I really didn't know.

Time would tell, I supposed.

Sweet and tangy, the ketchup dripped from my French fries until I shoved them in my mouth and licked the salt from my fingers. "Oh, puppies from Hades, this is good," I mumbled around the mouthful, reaching for the pop and taking a long pull on the straw. Bubbles exploded all the way down my throat, and I made a happy *mmmm* even as I was reaching for another fry. They were cut thick and had been cooked to perfection. I jammed another one in my mouth. I hadn't eaten in so long, it was as if I were starving.

Suddenly I realized that no one was saying anything, and I looked up. Shoe was sitting across from me in the booth. Nakita was to his right, her red purse sitting carefully on the table beside her. Barnabas was to my left, and beside him, Ace sat in sullen silence against the wall, holding a wad of ice wrapped in brown napkins to his head.

"What?" I asked, seeing that everyone was staring at me.

Nakita glanced at Barnabas, then said softly, "I've never seen you eat . . . like that."

My reach for another fry slowed, and I ate it in two bites instead of one. It was late, and the diner was empty but for us, the waitress counting money in the till, and the cook glowering at us through the hole in the wall, clearly wanting to go home. "I'm starving," I said, taking a tiny sip of pop when what I wanted to do was gulp it. "And tired." *But no heartbeat. None at all.*

Beside me, Barnabas leaned back in the bench seat, casual as he stirred the ice in his untouched drink. "It's kind of gross, Madison."

I eyed him, reading a soft envy in his carefully relaxed pose. "Jealous?" I asked tartly.

"Sort of," he muttered, looking up and away to where Grace and her new friend were chatting on the light fixture, their wings making them into softball-size globes of light only I and my reapers could see.

Eating another fry, I grimaced when a splotch of ketchup hit my lab coat. "I think it's from the flash forward," I said as I dabbed at it. "I was alive again, or at least it felt like I was when I was in Ace." I looked at him, feeling my face twist up in distaste. "You're a piece of work, you know that?"

The guy sneered at me, and, wadding up my napkin, I stifled

a yawn. "My mind must have remembered what it's like to be hungry. And tired. What time is it?"

Not looking, Barnabas said, "Midnight."

"Mmmm." I crumpled the napkin up and dropped it on the fries. I was still hungry, but I didn't want to look like a pig. "I gotta get home." It wasn't too late yet to call my mom as I had promised, school night or not. She kept hours like a vampire.

My gaze went back to Ace, scrunched up and silent in the corner of the booth. He hadn't said anything much since waking up in his truck. As it stood, there was not going to be any problem at the hospital come six the next morning. No one would ever know. What would happen to Ace now was anyone's guess.

Shoe, on the other hand . . . I smiled at him as he carefully felt his jaw, which was now turning an ugly purple. "You going to be okay?" I asked him, and he winced.

"I'm going to catch hell for trashing the school's computers," he said, glancing at Ace. "But I knew that before I did it. It's staying out to midnight on a school night that I wasn't planning on. But at this point, I don't care."

We all looked at Ace, who flipped us off. The waitress must have seen, because she cleared her throat loudly and went to talk to the cook in the kitchen.

I looked at the plate of fries, then ate one, feeling guilty for no reason that I could fathom. "Barnabas, maybe we can stop at Shoe's house on the way home and make his mom and dad think he's been tucked into bed," I suggested.

Barnabas nodded, looking a bit too casual for my comfort. Sneaky, almost.

"That'd be great," Shoe said nervously, edging away from Nakita as she started to mutter about wanting to just scythe the lot of them. But Shoe's discomfort seemed to be stemming from Barnabas's sly demeanor, not from Nakita, and I wondered if he was worried that I was going to go back on my word and change his memories as well.

Throwing his wad of damp napkins down, Ace sat straighter. "You all suck," he said loudly. "You're going to fix it so that no one remembers he's even been out?"

"Quiet!" Nakita hissed, leaning across the table. "You should be dead."

"You shut up!" he exclaimed, his brow furrowed. "Crazy chick!"

"Don't call me that!" she said, starting to rise, but when the guardian angel set her wings to humming, Nakita sat back down with a huff. "You're lucky, human," she muttered. "Lucky."

Lucky wasn't the word I'd like to apply to Ace, but he was. He'd tried to make a name for himself by killing people and blaming Shoe for it, and the only way he'd get in trouble for it now would be if Shoe got in bigger trouble, too. I was all for being honest and taking one's licks, but sometimes . . . the better part of valor and all.

Sighing, I slid to the end of the bench and stood. It was time to go home, and I dropped my head as I looked at the lab coat. I kind of liked it, even with the ketchup. Maybe I could start a new trend at school. I hadn't done anything really kooky yet to make myself stand out. Other than being dead, that is, and no one but Josh knew that. It would have been nice for him to have helped me tonight, and I missed him.

"We have to go," I said softly, giving my fries a last longing look.

Barnabas gathered himself, standing when Nakita did. The two of them exchanged knowing looks as they slid out of the booth. Their eyes had both gone silver, and I jumped to get in front of Shoe. "Not Shoe," I said, hand outstretched to keep them from wiping his memory.

Barnabas rolled his eyes. "Madison . . ." he started, but a subtle prickling in my temple shocked through me. Barnabas felt it, too, and so did Nakita.

"There once was a keeper named Ron," Grace said from the light fixtures, "whose karma was kind of a yawn. He showed up too late; some say it was fate. I think he's just really stupid, myself."

True, it didn't rhyme, but I still kind of liked it. "Ron is coming?" I said, bothered. *What does he want? It's over!*

"But I'm shielding us!" Nakita said, clearly bewildered.

"Apparently not well enough," Barnabas said snidely, and I felt all the more tired. Swell. They were arguing again.

"I won't let him mess with you," Grace said, and I smiled

up at her darting ball of light as she left the fixture. I knew my face still held my grateful expression when Shoe whistled and I followed his gaze to the front door, where Ron was standing just inside as if he'd been there all the time. Paul was standing beside him, and the little entry bells were not ringing.

Ron looked peeved, one hand lost in the folds of his flowing tunic as he put it on his hip and gestured at me with the other as if I were an errant child. I glared right back, shifting to hide Shoe, still sitting down. Barnabas moved to my right, Nakita to my left. Ron's gaze lingered over her traditional white clothes of a dark reaper, and Nakita lifted her chin.

"I wouldn't have believed it if I'd not seen it," Ron said, his eyes taking in my lab coat and yellow sneakers with their skulls. "The scything is over. The mark is safe. Well, he's beaten up, but he's alive," he added, glancing up at the two guardian angels. "I won. It's over. You lost. Go home, Madison."

I took a slow breath to find my words. *Mark,* I thought, deciding that giving people labels was degrading. "Ace has a name," I said softly, wondering how bad I looked when I noticed Paul was staring at me.

"Hi, Ron," I finally said loudly. "Come any closer, and I'm going to kick you right in your pendulum. What do you want? As you said, you already won."

The small man harrumphed, squinting warily first at the two guardian angels, then at my reapers flanking me, and finally at Ace behind us. "The seraphs sent me to adjust your amulet," he said, surprising me. "Me. Ha. Go figure. Apparently you're touching the divine too closely."

I'm touching the divine too closely? That was exactly what it had felt like. Maybe the hell I'd just gone through wasn't the norm.

Seeing me looking at him like I'd taken a week's worth of stupid pills, Ron strode forward among the empty tables with his usual quickness, halting with a comical abruptness when Barnabas flung out a hand in warning and Nakita suddenly had her sword out. The waitress made a muffled yelp, ducking into the back and babbling for the phone.

Better and better.

Ron stopped, his expression frustrated as he assessed the situation. Barnabas calmly crossed his ankles and leaned back against the table, looking good in his casual tee and black jeans. "You're not touching her . . . Chronos," the reaper said calmly, softly, his voice heavy with threat.

Ron's wrinkles grew deeper. "Back off. Her predecessor is dead. Who else is going to tweak her amulet? You? I'm here as the superior timekeeper under seraph orders. You think I'm going to violate those? How else could I find you, shielded as you are?"

On my other side, Nakita steamed, her grip on her sword hilt tightening. "You might if you thought you could get away with it," she said, and Paul, almost forgotten, inched forward.

"You're not superior, Ron. You're just older," I said, then

glanced at Paul, wondering. He'd helped me until Nakita had hit him. My guess was that he was going to have a black eye by morning. He'd never believe me again. I weighed the chances that Ron would do something sneaky against the real chance that my amulet wasn't tuned properly. I didn't want to go through that hell again, and I didn't want a seraph down here to fix it instead. Ron didn't look tired or distressed, and he had been flashing forward, too. Clearly something was wrong with me . . . again.

"He's right; it's over," I said, taking my amulet off and tossing it to Ron.

The silver-wrapped stone smacked into Ron's hand. Barnabas stiffened, and Nakita almost had kittens, falling to my side and finding an aggressive stance. It was a bold move on my part, but I was trying to prove to Ron that I wasn't afraid of him. Even if I was. I'd never have done it if I didn't have two reapers and two guardian angels standing by. I didn't think I could bear another look at the stars, raw and unfiltered, seen through the divine. "Just fix it," I said with a sigh, feeling naked without my amulet. "I can't take more than two flash forwards like that."

"Two?" Ron said, the amulet forgotten in his hands. "There was more than one?"

I smiled at him, lips closed. From the back, I could hear a frantic conversation, but at least the cook hadn't come out with a loaded shotgun. Yet. Barnabas and Nakita exchanged a look, and, sighing dramatically, the dark reaper slunk to the kitchen door. She hesitated, then dissolved her sword. Hair tossed back, she pushed on the double door and went in. Screaming quickly ensued, and we all waited until the twin thumps came before we turned back to one another.

Looking at Barnabas, Ron inched forward and extended my amulet. "You have to be wearing it for me to adjust it," he said.

I waited until Nakita came out before I stepped from Barnabas. A quick glance back at Shoe and I frowned. He looked scared. Breath held, I looped the simple cord around my neck, then stiffened when Ron took the stone in his fingers. I had trusted him once. Never again.

My jaw relaxed as a reddish light leaked from my amulet. The slight headache I didn't even realize I had lifted from me, and I exhaled, no longer feeling like I needed to hold myself together.

Ron's hand slipped from my amulet. Barnabas cleared his throat, clearly wanting me to step back near him, but I didn't, and it was Ron who moved first, with a new wariness in his stance. "Thanks," I said dryly. "I appreciate that."

Looking uncomfortable, Ron glanced at Paul, then at Shoe. "I adjusted your pull on the divine," he said gruffly. "Your predecessor was alive. You're not. It's going to take some tweaking." Wiping his hands together, he backed up. "I don't know what you had hoped to do by this. You made a bloody mess of it. How many people need their memories adjusted?"

Shoe scuffed his feet, and I shifted to hide him. "A few," I said. "And a few more now that you're butting in again. We can take care of it. And what do you mean, a bloody mess? It looks to me like I fixed it. No one died."

Paul edged forward to stand beside Ron as the older man pointed rudely at me. "Your job makes you a *murderer*, Madison," he said, and Barnabas stiffened. "Perhaps not with your own hands, but by your actions. Attempting to soothe your conscience by trying to save people whose souls are not even in danger only makes a mess and is an exercise in futility."

An exercise in futility? I thought, my chin lifting as I took a step forward. "I've died once, and trust me, the people we just saved would have wanted it that way." I was almost in his face, and I jumped when Barnabas pulled me back. "We saved three people's lives," I said from the security of his grip. "Four if you count Shoe not taking the blame for Ace's actions. They're *all* going to feel the sun on their faces tomorrow." Crap, I was almost crying again. "That feels good to me!" I finished hotly, wiping my eyes and not caring if Ron saw it.

And I did feel good. Sure, there was the problem of the flash forwards, but I didn't think I'd be living nightmares like tonight again. My amulet had needed adjusting. *Thank you, God, for sending Ron.*

"Maybe it was their time to go and you messed it up," Ron said as he glanced past the night-blackened windows, clearly thinking about leaving.

I smiled at him, thinking that for all his years, I'd been somewhere he hadn't. Maybe that was why I'd been fated to become the dark timekeeper. "That's fate, Ron, and you don't believe in fate. Or do you?"

His attention came back from the parking lot as he realized I'd basically said what a seraph had told him not two months ago. "Fine, you win," I said. "Congratulations. That worthless pile over there in the corner is safe. Got an angel and everything. Nothing to stop you from leaving. We've got a lot of cleanup to do." My thoughts went to the two people in the kitchen. "People to give memories to," I added, and Shoe cleared his throat behind me.

"Fate is an excuse," Ron blurted. "You don't know what people will choose. Ace might have changed someday without all this."

"Wrong!" I barked, and Paul's expression became pensive. "But I'm not going to argue with you. Whether you accept it or not, I believe in choice as much as you do. But that pile of shepherd dung," I said, pointing to Ace, who was hearing everything but ignoring us as he nursed his hurts, "wasn't going to change without some heavy intervention. He might now, but not the way you left him, knowing he had a guardian angel and a get-out-of-death-free card."

Paul's ears went red. Ron turned to him with a hush of sliding fabric.

"Will you just leave?" I said, retreating to Barnabas. "And

take your spying apprentice with you," I added.

Paul's mouth fell open at my caustic words, but I winked at him when Ron glanced away, and Grace giggled.

"You should give him more respect. He knows more than you do," Ron said as he drew Paul closer to him, and Barnabas snorted.

"I think he knows more than *you* do, Ron," I said. "Go already. And don't let the scythe hit you on the way out."

Nakita was fidgeting beside me, but I gave it little thought as Ron turned. "Come on, Paul," he said in a low, dangerous voice.

Suddenly, Nakita blurted, "I'm sorry I hit you, rising timekeeper," and both Barnabas and I jerked. She was red, and at our blank looks, she added, "What? I'm sorry. Can't I apologize?"

Stoic and silent, Ron simply vanished. Paul, though, was still here. His sandals scuffing the tile, Paul looked at the empty space beside him where Ron had been. "Um," he mumbled as his attention came back to us. "Thanks, Nakita. It's okay."

"You know I said that only to get him off your case, right?" I said, and Paul touched his nose, smiling before he vanished as well in a shining line of light.

With a heavy exhale, Shoe fell back onto the bench seat, muttering.

Barnabas took his seat as well, thoughtful. "Did you notice the rising timekeeper's amulet is the same color as mine?" he asked.

"Really?" I said, but then the oddity of Barnabas's question hit me, and I turned to him. "Is that important?"

Startled out of his thoughts, Barnabas looked everywhere but at me. "It should be shifting up the spectrum to red." The reaper's eyes landed on mine. "I bet Ron isn't happy about that."

My lips parted as I wondered what that might mean, but Barnabas cleared his throat and looked to the silent kitchen. "We need to go. Nakita, are the cook and the waitress set?"

Nakita was taking a picture of the dusty light fixture, holding the camera at a very odd angle. "They're fine," she said as she looked at the screen. "Where's your wallet, Madison?" she asked. "Still in the truck?"

"Oh, yeah!" I said, turning back to my plate of food. "My phone is out there, too." But when I looked at the golden, crispy fries, my reach for them hesitated. Slowly my smile evaporated, replaced by a feeling of despair.

"I'm not hungry anymore!" I wailed, and Nakita blinked at me. "Don't you get it?" I cried, looking down at my amulet. "I was eating because my amulet wasn't working right. Ron fixed it, and now I'm not hungry anymore!"

"Thank God for small favors," Barnabas muttered as he pulled himself upright. "It was really gross, Madison."

Depressed, I sank back down. "But I like eating," I said mournfully. Darn it, it wasn't fair! Unhappy, I fingered a French fry. Grace dropped down, warming my hand as she offered condolences the only way she could—until she thought up a poem, that was.

"There once was a girl who liked fries," Grace started, and Barnabas made an exasperated sound.

"Your wallet, Madison?" Nakita offered.

"Yeah, right." I muttered, and I stood.

"Sorry, Madison," Shoe said, clearly not understanding why fries were so important to me, but knowing I was upset.

"It's okay." Head down, I angled toward the door, slowing as my amulet seemed to grow heavy, warm almost, but a sudden thought pulled me to a stop. How had Nakita known my wallet was in the truck?

Suspicious, I spun back to the table, my guess borne out when I saw Barnabas's eyes had silvered.

"What . . . wait!" I exclaimed, lurching back to the table. "Shoe! Don't look at him!"

Barnabas's head swiveled to me. A drop of fear slid through me at his alien eyes, silver and glowing with a holy light. Across the table from him, Shoe gasped, breaking the grip Barnabas had on him and dropping his head. Ace was already staring vacantly, his lips parted, clearly still under Barnabas's influence.

"Madison!" Barnabas barked, eyes still glowing as Shoe rubbed his face and blinked.

I tugged Shoe up and out of the booth. "Not Shoe," I said. "I promised him he could remember."

Barnabas's jaw clenched and his brow furrowed. "Madison . . ." he grumbled, his eyes again a steady brown.

"Yeah, that's my name," I said hotly. "Mad Madison. I say Shoe can remember, and I'm your boss."

Grace made a long *oooooh* sound, and the second guardian angel on the light fixture went quiet, her wings stilling to make her vanish. Barnabas's eyes narrowed as he turned in the seat and looked me up and down. "No, you're not," he said, and Nakita scuffed her feet behind me. "I'm grim. Anytime I want, I'm out of here."

He wouldn't, I thought, panicking. "Oh, yeah?" I said, almost daring him.

"Yeah," Barnabas said, clearly not happy.

Beside me, Shoe looked frightened. I took a slow breath, trying to find some way to keep from alienating Barnabas. He'd been there when I had died, tried to save me, believed in me. I trusted him, and he was probably the only person who might really understand me.

"Yeah," I said more softly. "Okay. I'm sorry. You're right. I'm not your boss." I turned to Nakita, seeing her eyes wide and frightened. "Nakita, I'm not yours, either, but this is my scythe, and I want Shoe to remember."

"Yes, you are," Nakita said immediately, the surety of her voice making Shoe frown. "I'm sworn to your will and your bidding."

I was sooooo glad that Ace was out of it. It was embarrassing enough having Shoe hear this. "My being your boss is not the world I want to live in," I said, trying to make her understand. Pleading now, I looked back to the table. "Barnabas, I told Shoe I'd let him remember tonight. Please."

"I didn't promise him," he said tightly, but the anger directed toward me was gone.

"Please," I tried again.

Barnabas seemed to grow smaller as he exhaled, hands gesturing loosely. "I can't let him run around knowing what happened! It just isn't done!"

"Why not?" I asked bluntly. "How are people supposed to make a change in their lives if they don't remember? Dreams? That's poppycock."

"Poppycock?" Nakita echoed, clearly confused.

"I want Shoe and Ace both to remember," I decided suddenly. "No fake memories for either of them."

Barnabas looked at Ace, who was still blinking stupidly at nothing. "No!" he exclaimed, pointing a finger at me, which made the guardian angels above whisper among themselves, making bets as to how this was going to end. "Not going to happen," he added loudly, glowering up at them as they giggled. "It's the rules, Madison."

I stared at him, the fingers of one hand making a slow roll of sound against the tabletop.

"Stare all you want," Barnabas said, not looking at me. "I'm clearing their memories."

Taking Shoe's elbow, I moved him to stand behind me.

"Uh, Barnabas?" Nakita finally said. "I don't think saying no to the dark timekeeper is a good idea, even if she's wrong. She's going to be able to stop time eventually."

Behind me, Shoe said softly, "I want to remember."

"Memory is all we have," I said, trying to make Barnabas understand. "It's why we make the choices we do. How do you expect anyone to change if you smother the past in a lie?"

Slowly Barnabas's jaw unclenched, and I felt a stirring of victory. "It's going to cause problems," he warned, and I straightened, smiling.

"So what?" I said flippantly. "Shoe won't say anything." I spun to him. "Will you?"

Shoe was shaking his head, still worried. "No one would believe me. Grim reapers? Guardian angels? Timekeepers? They'd lock me up."

From my other side, Nakita coaxed, "Timekeepers change for a reason, Barnabas. That's all Madison seems to do. Change, change, change."

Barnabas frowned again. "Get him out of here," he muttered, and, elated, I grabbed Shoe's arm, wondering if Barnabas was only pacifying me, planning on coming back later, when I wouldn't know about it.

"What about Ace?" I asked, feeling ten feet tall.

"Out," Barnabas said tightly. "You got Shoe. Ace is not an option."

I took a breath to argue, then hesitated when Ace's guardian angel circled Grace twice and flew to me, whispering, "Grace says, 'There once was a boy in a diner, who thought no one else could be finer. He wasn't that kind, almost lost his mind, till an angel became his reminder.'"

Oh, really?

Barnabas raised his eyebrows suspiciously, and, refusing to answer his unspoken question, I began backing up, stumbling when our locked gazes were broken. "Come on," I breathed to Shoe. "I have to get my wallet." Grabbing his hand, I tugged him to the door.

"What about Ace?" he asked, looking behind him until I turned his head away.

"Don't look. I think Ace will be okay," I said as the door jingled open and Nakita sighed loudly. "His guardian angel is going to block Barnabas."

Shoe twisted to look through the plate-glass windows. "Are you sure?"

It was cooler out here, and I was glad for the lab coat as I held my arms around myself and waited. I wasn't cold—but if I had been alive, I would have been.

"I've been told cherubs sit next to God," I said, looking up at the stars and smiling. "I think a guardian angel can beat Barnabas's skills with a stick."

Shoe's cough brought my attention down, and in the buzz of the security light, I met his startled gaze. "Really?"

he stammered, glancing into the diner and then back to me. "Cherubs, eh?"

I shrugged. "Grace is. Just promise me you won't say anything about tonight."

Head down, he smiled as he scuffed his toe into the broken sidewalk. "You want me to lie?"

I couldn't help my grin. "Well, I am the *dark* timekeeper."

A twinge tightened across my mind, and my amulet grew warm, then cold. It was Barnabas using his amulet, and I glanced in as he leaned toward Ace. I wasn't surprised when Ace woke up, his empty look shifting to hatred as he exclaimed, "You can go to hell, reaper!"

Barnabas looked out the window at me, cross. "Madison!" he complained.

Nakita laughed, the sound coming faintly through the glass. "I told you! Don't mess with her."

Smiling, I turned away. Shoe was standing in front of me, his hands in his pockets. "I don't want to forget this," Shoe said wistfully. "I don't want to forget any of it."

"You won't," I said confidently, and with a sudden idea, I leaned back against the brick wall of the restaurant to untie my sneaker. Shoe watched in confusion until I got the lace entirely undone, pulling it from my yellow sneaker with a rasping sound. "Here," I said, handing it to him. "To remember everything by." I was breathless, and I didn't even need to breathe. What if he thought I was weird or something?

But Shoe grinned, and I exhaled in relief. "Thanks," he said, taking it. "I, um, don't have— Wait," he said, digging in his pocket. "Here," he said, handing me a coupon from the Chicken Coop. "It's not like I expect you to use it," he said, red-faced. "But the only other thing I've got on me is my driver's license."

I smiled, looking at it in the dim light. "Bye, Shoe," I said as I rocked back. "Have a great life. Be good. Make good choices." I lifted the coupon. "Thanks."

He closed his mouth, looking embarrassed and pleased all at once. "I'll try," he finally said, then frowned as he looked at Ace through the glass. "It's not going to be easy."

I laughed as I started to walk backward to Ace's truck, each step feeling bigger than it really was. "If being good were easy, everyone would do it."

Shoe nodded. Waving awkwardly, he turned and began walking down the dark sidewalk, his pace slow but gaining confidence with every step until his head was high. Slowly the darkness took him until even the sound of his shoes echoing back to me faded and there was nothing.

I saw him once more in a spot of light, and then . . . he was gone.

Satisfaction filled me as I yanked open Ace's truck and got my phone and wallet. The soft leather was still warm from the ride over here, and it made an uncomfortable bump when I shoved it in a back pocket. The door squeaked as I slammed it shut. In the distance, I heard a faint, "Bye, Madison!"

Happy, I leaned against the truck and stared at the plain white stars while I waited for Nakita and Barnabas to finish threatening Ace. Sure, Barnabas might be mad at me, but he'd get me home, grumbling all the way. If he didn't, Nakita would. Even better, he'd be on my roof tomorrow to tell me what I could have done better. No one had died tonight. No one would die tomorrow—at least, not before their allotted time was up. Shoe was going to catch hell at school, but he'd known that before he trashed the school's computers. Nakita was starting to understand—I think—even if by all accounts she had failed in her attempt to save Ace's soul by taking it early. Ace was still an ass, but maybe he'd learned something. Paul was thinking. And I was . . . pleasantly tired.

Maybe it was a good night after all.

Epilogue

"Madison!"

It was a panicked shout, and my eyes flew open at the strong shake of my shoulder.

"What!" I shouted back, seeing my dad standing over me, fear on his face. I was in my bed; the sun was shining in. I had been . . . sleeping? I hadn't slept in almost three months.

Relief cascaded over my dad's face to make his few wrinkles appear deeper. "I thought you were—" he started, then visibly changed his mind as he let go of my shoulder and straightened. "You're late," he said instead, sounding embarrassed. "For school," he added, and I smiled. I hadn't thought he meant the dead kind of late, but then again, I'd probably looked dead, lying there. Not breathing. No wonder he'd shaken me.

"How late?" I asked as I sat up, blinking. I couldn't believe

I'd actually slept. Maybe the flash forward had triggered it. It had taken a lot out of me.

Exhaling, my dad looked over my room. "Breakfast is ready," he said instead of answering me.

Too bad I wasn't hungry.

I started to get up, then froze when he picked up the lab coat I'd draped over my desk chair. The Jane Doe toe tag was peeping out of the pocket, and I panicked. How was I going to explain a clearly professional lab coat with the name Marty on it was beyond me.

"Tell me this is ketchup," he said softly, fingering the stained fabric, and I smiled.

"It's ketchup. I had some fries after school," I explained, and he sighed. "I'm sorry! I got hungry!"

He winced, draping it over my desk chair, right next to my torn tights.

"Madison!" he said, snatching them up. "What did you do to your nylons?"

"I cut them. Everyone is wearing them like that!" Oh, man. I was not getting out of this.

"These were brand-new!" my dad complained loudly, shaking them.

"Jeez, Dad . . ." I complained, proud of myself that I hadn't panicked. Much. "Didn't you ever wear cutoff jeans?"

Shoulders slumping, he looked at my fingernails, seeing the black nails that I'd been wearing to help Nakita blend in, his gaze lingering on the two red nails I'd half painted. "Torn tights and a lab coat? Wearing shoes without laces? I'll never understand your fashion sense."

I leaned over to look at my yellow sneakers. *It isn't fashion sense; it's fallout,* I thought dryly.

"But at least I know you're eating," he added, his attention going back to the ketchup-splattered lab coat. "How about skipping the after-school snacks for a while and eating at home?"

"Okay." I stretched, hoping he wouldn't look into my bathroom, where my torn shirt lay on the floor. *That* would be very hard to explain. I felt pretty good, but food was the last thing on my mind. Especially when my dad sat on the edge of the bed beside me and pointedly set my phone on the nightstand.

Crap. I'd forgotten to call Mom.

"Anything you want to tell me?" he asked, looking at it.

"Sorry. I forgot to call Mom," I said immediately, but his frown deepened, telling me that wasn't it. Clueless, I fiddled with my comforter, glad I'd changed into my nightgown last night after Barnabas had dropped me off, even if it had put my torn tights and Marty's lab coat on my dad's radar. "Is something wrong?" I asked hesitantly.

Is something wrong? I actually asked, "Is something wrong"? Can I sound any guiltier?

My dad waited until I looked at him. "I got a strange call this morning. Some guy named Sneaker."

"Shoe!" I blurted before I remembered to shut my mouth. For

crying out loud. And I'd told Shoe to be good when I couldn't go five minutes without lying to my dad?

"Shoe?" my dad echoed, touching the phone to make it exactly square with the corner of the nightstand. "You know him?"

"Uh, yes." I shrugged, trying to look like I didn't care. "But I never gave him the house number." *Barnabas?* I thought. Had he gone to see Shoe last night and tried to change his memories? Son of a dead puppy.

"Pen pal?" I tried, working to keep the question from my voice, but it sneaked in there somehow.

My dad made an unconvincing sound. "He wanted me to tell you he's suspended and that he is, and I quote, 'being good.'" His eyebrows high, he waited for an explanation.

"Really?" What else could I say? I couldn't look at him, and I fidgeted in the silence.

"Madison . . ." he started, and I threw the covers back to get out of bed on the other side.

"Dad, I gotta go," I blurted, reaching for my robe just inside my bathroom. The sight of my torn shirt met me, and I yanked the door shut. "I'm late for school and I have to take a shower. I don't know why Shoe said that weird stuff. He's just a guy I met a while ago."

Like last night, a while ago, but it was a while ago.

Exhaling slowly and long, my dad stood. "I'll see you downstairs," he said, sounding disappointed. "What do you want for dinner tonight?"

I hesitated, thinking what I could hide in my pockets the easiest. "Soup and fries," I said, imagining that I could down soup easily enough. And I had really enjoyed the fries last night. If I could save Ace's life, I could eat a couple.

My dad's expression screwed up. "Soup and fries?" he echoed, then sighed. "If that's what you want. Breakfast is ready. Don't be long."

"I won't," I said, thinking that if I waited until the last moment to come down, I could run out the door with a piece of toast to give to Sandy. Smiling, I waved to my dad when he stood in the hall, and I shut the door. I mentally kicked myself as I listened to his steps clump down the stairs. I'd *waved* to him? I was so *stupid*!

I hadn't been lying about wanting to take a shower, and, still worried, I went into my bathroom to get the water started as I wiggled out of my pj's. A soft tap on my bathroom door made me snatch a towel, and I called through the door, "I'll be right down, Dad!"

But it wasn't my dad who said, "Uh, Madison?"

I froze. Worried, I cracked the door open.

"You!" I shouted, flinging the door wide when I saw Paul standing in the middle of my room, my window shoved all the way open and the screen propped up against the wall. "What are you doing here?" I almost hissed as I stormed out, slowing down when I remembered I was in a towel. "You can't just pop in like this! My dad's downstairs. If he saw you up here, he'd have kittens!"

Paul turned red, and he fidgeted with his button-down shirt tucked into a pair of black slacks. His clothes were still kind of straitlaced, but at least he wasn't dressed like an actor in a space opera anymore. "Sorry," he said, not looking at me, seemingly fascinated with my carpet. "I wanted to ask you something, and Ron doesn't let me off the leash much."

"What?" I snapped, feeling very naked under my big fluffy towel.

Paul glanced at me, then up to the ceiling. "You believe in choice?"

I hesitated, my anger sputtering out. "Yes," I said softly. He had helped me. I owed him a few answers.

"But you're the dark timekeeper," Paul stated, sounding confused.

"Apparently," I said dryly, then added, "It doesn't make sense, but that's the way it is. As soon as I find my body, I'm out of here. Unless . . . I can change things."

Paul's shiny shoes shifted on my carpet. "You don't want to be a timekeeper?"

My thoughts returned to the awful feeling of helplessness when I had flashed forward, and then my elation when Shoe had walked away, his entire life ahead of him. "I don't know anymore."

"Maybe you just got my job," Paul said, surprising me.

Surprised, I leaned against the doorframe, then pushed

myself up. No matter how much I tried, I'd never look confident dressed in a towel. "You believe in fate?" I asked.

Paul made a face, backing up to sit on the open window's sill. "I don't know what I believe. But Ron left when Ace got his guardian angel, and you stuck around to try to save people's lives."

I tightened my grip on my towel, not knowing what to say.

"I gotta go," Paul said as he stood. "I'm supposed to be practicing my jumps, but if I'm not back when he thinks I should be, he tracks me down."

"Must be nice having a teacher," I said, more than a little jealous and not wanting him to leave yet. "You didn't come all the way over here to ask me if I believed in choice."

Paul lifted a shoulder and let it fall in a half shrug. "No. I thought you might like to know that Ron did a far-seeing search on both of them and found that neither Ace nor Shoe is fated to drop any more viruses. In fact, Shoe eventually goes to work for the CIA and tracks down other hackers. He's probably the one who prevents a cyber terrorist attack at the turn of the decade. Right now Ace is in a padded room because he's talking about reapers and timekeepers, but he eventually learns to keep his mouth shut, gets out of rehab, starts a band called Melting Crows, and dies of a drug overdose in his thirties."

"Oh, man. That's awful," I whispered, wondering if it had been worth it.

Paul was unperturbed. "Everyone dies eventually. His music

will touch people," he said. "Get them to think. If you ask me, his guardian angel is probably screaming in his ear right now, trying to get him to hear her. Ace never becomes a saint, but his life will have meaning. At least, I think so."

"I suppose," I said, still not comfortable with it. Maybe I should have let Nakita kill him. End it cleanly. Were unfinished souls given a second chance? Another go-round? Was that why light reapers took them early? "Were you the one who gave Shoe my home phone number?" I asked suddenly.

Paul put a hand on my window frame as if to leave. "He wanted to tell you he was okay. I didn't think you'd mind, and since I don't have your cell phone number, I looked up your home number. I didn't mess with him, if that's what you're worried about. Ron is pissed." Paul smirked, his gaze leaving mine as he remembered. "The guardian angel I gave Ace won't let anyone tamper with his or Shoe's memories. That's why he did the far search on them."

Another worry was put to rest, and when Paul went to step out, I blurted, "Thank you for stopping Ace."

Head cocked, he smiled to show his teeth. "You're welcome."

From downstairs, my dad shouted for me, and I shifted from foot to foot. "I gotta go," I said, tossing my head to the shower steaming behind me.

"Me too," he said, stepping over my windowsill and onto the roof.

"Do you like Ron?" I asked suddenly, and he hesitated, searching the corners of my room with his gaze.

"I don't know," he said softly. "He teaches me stuff, but it's like he's fanatic about you."

His eyes found mine, and I nodded. "He lied to me. A lot. I made him look bad in front of a seraph. You going to keep believing everything he says?"

Paul didn't answer, ducking his head and smiling. "See you later," he said, and then the shadows from the tree branches shifting on him seemed to erase him bit by bit until he was gone.

I stood for a moment to be sure he had left. "I have *got* to learn how to do that," I whispered, then went to take my shower.

Ace becomes a musician, eh? I thought, smiling as I imagined how it must rankle Ron that I—a dark timekeeper—had shown the lost a new choice, and that that choice had been made because of our efforts, saving not only his soul, but his life.

Had it all been fate? Or sweet reaper justice?

Early to Death, Early to Rise

Character close-ups for the living, the dead, and everything in between

---

Madison's glossary to the world of angels and reapers

A sneak peek at how Madison's destiny (or something like it) unfolds in Kim Harrison's third and final book in the Madison Avery trilogy, *Something Deadly This Way Comes*

Character close-ups for the living, the dead, and everything in between

Name: Madison Avery
Status: Dead (and not loving it), with the illusion of a body courtesy of a strange amulet stolen from her killer
Skills: It's still a mystery, but there is something powerful right below the surface.
Favorite Saying: "Puppy presents on the rug!"

Name: Josh Daniels
Status: Alive and getting cuter by the minute
Skills: Does being cute count? If not, then how about being decent at track?
Favorite Saying: "It was just a dream, right?"

Name: Barnabas
Status: Light reaper assigned to prevent Madison's death, which obviously did not go as planned
Skills: The ability to alter human memories
Favorite Saying: "Madison, you have no idea the trouble you've caused!"

Name: Guardian, Reaper-Augmented Cherub, Extinction Security (G.R.A.C.E.S. one-seventy-six), aka Grace
Status: First-sphere guardian angel assigned to keep Madison away from trouble—an impossible task
Skills: A field of immunity that protects those around her (and a way with annoying limericks)
Favorite Saying: "I'm a guardian angel, not a miracle worker."

Name: Chronos, Ron for short
Status: Light timekeeper who lives on earth and believes only in free will
Skills: The ability to manipulate time—and people
Favorite Saying: "Oh, look at the time. I must be off."

Name: Nakita
Status: Dark reaper with supermodel looks and a taste for scything
Skills: The ability to ruthlessly end people's lives before they have a chance to turn evil . . . but somewhat lacking in people skills
Favorite Saying: "I will rip out your tongue and feed it to my hellhounds!"

Name: Kairos, aka Seth, the sexy senior who killed Madison (right after he kissed her, mmmm)
Status: Previous dark timekeeper whose amulet is providing Madison with the illusion of a body
Skills: The ability to create amulets for reapers and angels, and to read the lines of time and figure out when a person is fated to turn bad. Oh, and he's a good kisser. . . .
Favorite Saying: "I will be immortal!"

Early to Death, Early to Rise Glossary

Now that she's dead, Madison has even more vocab to learn than she did in high school English. What's a black wing? What do amulets do, exactly? Here's what's on her flash cards in the afterlife.

Dark reapers: Reapers who Kairos sends to kill people when the probable future shows that they are going to make decisions contrary to the grand schemes of fate.

Light reapers: Reapers who Ron sends to save those people from an untimely death, to ensure humanity's right of free will.

Timekeepers: Both the light and dark reapers have their own timekeeper. Each one is responsible for watching the strands of time to determine when a person must be scythed—or saved.

Amulet: A stonelike necklace that makes it possible to communicate beyond the earth's sphere. Each amulet has its own aura or song that matches with its owner.

Black wings: Creatures that feed on the souls of those killed by dark reapers, typically appearing right before a scything takes place. Most of the time they go unnoticed by the living, but they can resemble crows when a soul is in danger.

A sneak peek at how Madison's destiny (or something like it) unfolds in Kim Harrison's third and final book in the Madison Avery trilogy, *Something Deadly This Way Comes*

Prologue

I'm Madison Avery, dark timekeeper in charge of heaven's hit squad . . . and fighting it all the way. Funny how timekeeper never popped up on my "careers good for you" when I did the test at school. The seraphs say I was born to the position, and when the choice was take the job or die? Well . . . I took the job.

"Fate," the seraphs would say. "Bad choice" if you ask me. Even now I don't believe in fate, and so I'm stuck working with a confused dark reaper who is trying to understand, and a light reaper twice fallen from heaven who thinks my ideas are a lost cause. Instead of just following orders sent down from above, I want to do things my own way, which involves trying to convince people to change. My only hope is to locate my real body so I can give the amulet back and forget the entire thing happened, because convincing heaven that I can save lost souls is looking impossible. It'd be a lot easier if my own people weren't working against me.

One

The hot sun seemed to go right through me, reflecting off the aluminum bleachers to warm me from my feet up as I stood beside Nakita and cheered Josh on. He was running the two-mile in an invitational, and they were doing the last bit right on the track. The front three runners had begun to pick up the pace for the last hundred yards. Josh was ahead, but the guy behind him had saved some push for the last bit, too.

"Go, Josh! Run! Run!" Nakita yelled, and surprised, I lowered my camera to look at her. The dark reaper didn't especially like Josh—she'd almost killed him once—and her excitement was unusual. Her pale face was flushed, and her eyes, usually a faded blue, were bright as she leaned forward and grasped the chain-link fence between us and the track. She was wearing a pink top with matching pink nail polish to hide her naturally black nails. Open-toed sandals and capris helped her blend in, and she looked nothing like one might imagine a dark reaper, capable of "smiting" lost souls.

I was dressing down today—at least for me—in jeans and a black, lacy top. My hair, though, was its usual purple-tipped cut, hanging around my ears, and I still wore my funky yellow sneakers with their new black laces with skulls on them. They matched my earrings.

"He's right behind you!" the angel in disguise shouted, and her matte-black amulet sparked violet at its core. More evidence she was excited. Shaking my head, I turned back to the race, bringing my camera up and focusing on the finish line. I snapped a picture for the school paper as Josh squeaked over the finish line. My smile was full of a quiet satisfaction that he'd won.

"He won! He won!" Nakita exclaimed, and I gasped when she pulled me into jumping up and down with her. I couldn't help but give her a hug back, breathless as I caught my balance. She certainly wasn't *acting* like one of heaven's hit squad, as excited as if she was Josh's girlfriend. Which she wasn't. I might be. Maybe.

"Barnabas." Nakita shoved his feet where he reclined two rows above us. "Josh won. Say something!"

The former light reaper pushed his hat up and gave her a dry look. "Whoopee," he said sarcastically, then pulled his long legs closer and sat up, squinting in the sun. "Madison, you were going to work with me today on hiding your amulet's resonance."

Grimacing, I looked down at the jet-black stone cradled by silver wires that I wore around my neck. Besides giving me the tactile illusion of a make-believe body, hiding me from black wings, and giving me my connection to the divine, my amulet sang. Sort of. Mimicking a natural aura, the black stone rang like a bell that only the divine could hear. Anyone who knew how to listen could find me in a second—be they friend or foe. Which might be a problem if I was out trying to keep my own people from killing someone, and which was why I needed to learn how to hide it. After hanging out with Josh, of course.

"She can do that later," Nakita said primly. "He won!"

I felt a twinge of guilt. I *had* promised to work with him after school, but I'd forgotten I'd also promised Ms. Cartwright I'd take pictures of the track meet for the school paper.

"Sorry," I said softly, and he shrugged, making no effort to hide his boredom.

For all his sour attitude, Barnabas had been on earth longer than Nakita and therefore had all the subtle nuances of human behavior to fit in with the track moms and cheering girlfriends better than Nakita. His lanky build and faded T-shirt only added to his sigh-worthy looks, but Barnabas truly didn't have a clue how good he looked. Nakita didn't know why guys followed her around looking for dates, either. That the two of them hung out with me had the popular cliques cross-eyed.

"This was his only race," I offered hesitantly, and Barnabas leaned back, stretching out on the warm bleacher to put his hat over his face.

Turning back to the track, I snapped a picture of Josh as he accepted the congratulations of his teammates. Sweat made patterns on his shirt, and his blond hair was dark with it. He was the only one apart from Barnabas and Nakita who knew I was technically dead; not only had he been there as I had died, but he had held my hand during the whole thing. Yep, I was dead: no heartbeat unless I got excited or scared, no need to eat—though I could do it in a pinch to fit in, and I hadn't had so much as a nap in months. It had been fun at first, but now I'd give just about anything to enjoy a juicy hamburger and crispy fries. Everything sort of tasted like rice cakes.

"I didn't know you liked sports," I said to Nakita as Josh waited for the runners to pass before crossing the track to talk to us through the fence.

"We have contests," she said. "This has the same appeal." Her gaze went from the runners to the moms chatting among themselves, barely conscious of the meet at all. "I came in third once, with the blade," she added.

Barnabas snickered, his face still hidden under his hat. "Real good with that scythe, eh?" he muttered, and she smacked his foot.

"And where did you place?" she asked him hotly.

Sitting up, Barnabas watched Josh, his eyes not seeing

him but the past. "They didn't have contests when I was in heaven."

I winced. Barnabas had been kicked out of heaven before the pyramids had been built.

"Sorry," Nakita said, surprising me with her downcast eyes. She usually took every opportunity to needle Barnabas about his fallen status. According to Nakita, Barnabas had been kicked out of heaven because he'd fallen in love with a human girl.

"Hi, Josh," I said as he scuffed to a halt behind the chain-link fence.

"Almost lost that one," he said, breathing heavily. When he smiled at me, I felt warm inside. We'd been dating for a while, and his smile still hit me hard. And his kisses, even more.

"But you didn't," Nakita said, back to her serious self again. "It was a good run."

Josh gave her a quizzical look, probably wondering at her earnest expression. "Thanks," he said, then wiped the sweat from his neck. I hadn't sweated in months. Not since I'd died.

"Is that your last race?" I asked, already knowing.

"Yup." Josh waved to the guy calling him from the finish line. "I gotta go, but do you want to go to The Low D with me later?" The Low D was the local hangout, short for The Lowest Common Denominator. Three Rivers was a college town, and the students got the joke even if no one else did. His eyes rose to take in Nakita and Barnabas. "All of you?" he added somewhat sourly.

It was hard to find the time to be alone with Josh between school, my dad, my job at the flower shop, and don't forget being the dark timekeeper, stealing every free moment of your day and night. One might think that not needing to sleep would give you tons of time, but it didn't.

Already guessing my answer, Barnabas sighed from under his hat. It was likely going to be after sundown before I practiced shielding my amulet's resonance. But a quiver went through me, and my heart, or at least the memory of it, gave a hard thump and went still. "Sure," I said, smiling. Small word, heavy in significance.

Josh stuck his fingers through the mesh, and I touched them. Josh and I had been through a lot together, especially considering our rocky start when I was his pity date at prom. We were doing good now, even with the dark timekeeper stuff butting in. Smiling with half his face and looking charmingly beguiling, Josh pulled back, finally turning to face his friends as he walked away. Nakita was scowling when I turned around.

"You promised Barnabas you'd practice," she said, surprising me.

"It's okay to put off practice to watch Josh run, but it's not okay if I want to socialize a little?" I asked.

"Absolutely."

It was reaper logic, and I knew I couldn't win. Sad thing was, she was probably right. Turning away, I sat on the bleachers to wait for Josh. Barnabas was behind me smelling of feathers and the back of clouds—and yes, the back of clouds do have a smell. Ignoring me, Nakita went to stand at the fence, watching the stragglers come in. I wondered if she ought to go out for cross-country, then squashed the idea. She was here to protect me from myself, not learn how to run the two-mile.

But all thoughts of practice and The Low D left me when, without warning, a blue ink seemed to pour from the sun, hitting the earth and boiling up like smoke. It bled across the ground, washing over people oblivious to it, turning me cold. In the time it took to pull my head up, the blue had risen to encompass everything.

Puppy presents on the rug. I'm going to flash forward.

My heart gave a pound and stopped as a quick wash of fear slid into me. The last time I'd flashed forward to see the future, I had cried at the stars and felt like I was going to die. Then I fell into someone else's mind and lived out the ugly moment when they began to kill their own soul. That had been almost a month ago, and I didn't know what scared me more: that I might have to live through that hell again, or that the seraphs were giving me another chance to prove that killing a person wasn't necessary to save their soul—and I might screw it up?

According to Grace—my annoying, often missing guardian angel and heavenly liaison—although the seraphs didn't cause my flash forwards, they could stop them or make them come early, sort of screen them to make my transition to a fully functioning dark timekeeper easier. It wasn't like I had a real teacher, having been dumped into the position. You'd think that the seraphs themselves would take on the job of assigning reaps permanently, but apparently angels had a hard time figuring out what was now, what was then, and what was to be, and it took a human to understand time. I happened to be in charge of the bad guys, the ones who killed people before they killed their souls. I'd rather be in charge of the light, who tried to stop the killing, but that's not what had happened.

Voices faded in and out through the blue mist as I waited for the future to take me. "Madison, you can practice at The Low D," Nakita said, kicking the fence to make it shudder. "The distraction will be good. Barnabas, it's no wonder she never learns anything with you, teaching her at midnight on her roof."

I clutched at my knees, terrified that if I moved, I'd find myself convulsing on the ground. The moment when a soul begins to die is traumatic, and it rings through the time lines and into the future, causing the flash forwards. The deeper into the future, the hazier the vision is, ranging from a crystal clarity to a murky nothing that only voices could penetrate. Which meant that if I was the first timekeeper to flash forward I didn't necessarily have the advantage. Ron, the light timekeeper, might flash later, but clearer, and pull the reap right out from under me.

"Guys?" I whispered, and then gasped when the entire track with its runners, coaches, and blue lawn chairs was suddenly superimposed with a scene that was possibly a hundred miles distant and probably days into the future. And though I clutched at the ribbed heat of the aluminum bench, I also stood on a chalk-decorated sidewalk, staring at a three-story apartment building with old cars out front and a busy road behind me, traffic at a standstill. There was fuzzy blue haze at the edges of my vision and around every person, like a second aura.

The night was an awful mix of orange and black as the building burned, flames leaping high to show clusters of neighbors huddled together, dogs barking, and people screaming. Fire trucks spewed air scented with diesel fuel to the curb, which billowed up and warmed my ankles. Roaring. Everything was roaring. And then I realized it was the blood in my head as heartache gripped me.

Johnny is still in there.

The thought echoed in our shared mind. Terror that belonged to the girl whose body I was in filled me, and I felt myself stand, wobbling on the bleachers. I was flashing forward, living someone else's nightmare. This was when her soul started to die, when something so bad happened that she forgot how to live. I was the only one who might be able to save her.

"Johnny!" I shouted, and Nakita turned to me. I could see her shock, and the image of a burning building grew behind her and melted into the reality of the track meet.

"She's flashing," I heard Barnabas say, and his hand clamped over my arm, keeping me from running forward as the girl whose mind I was in bolted.

In my vision, I ran through the cars, dodging firefighters trying to stop me, the blue haze rising from people like a fog. In reality, I felt my heart pound as I locked my knees and swayed so I wouldn't run as well. *I left Johnny alone. He was asleep. I waited until he was asleep after Mom left for work. Oh, God. Mom is going to kill me when she finds out! I don't understand. How can there be a fire?!*

"Johnny!" I whispered as the girl screamed, then jumped when a heavy hand clamped onto my arm, and both the girl and I turned.

I blinked, wavering when I saw Barnabas behind the frightening image of a fireman in full gear, his breath hissing as he tried to keep me from going in. The crowd in the bleachers was standing, cheering on the last of the runners fighting it out. In my vision, the fire screamed, a surreal counterpoint to the terror filling me. Barnabas's hand was on my arm, and he peered at me in sympathy.

"Johnny is in there!" I said, and the fireman stared, his expression hidden behind the face mask. "Let me go. Let me go! I have to get in there!"

As one, the girl and I twisted in Barnabas's/the fireman's grip, and as one, we were hoisted into their arms. I tried not to fight, knowing it wasn't real, but the girl's terror was mine.

I had no heart to beat in my solid, make-believe body, but memory is a funny thing, and I felt the echo of a pulse as Barnabas carried me, taking the jarring steps down the bleachers and to the cooler shade below. The night bathed my heated cheeks, scorched by sun and fire as Barnabas set me on the ground, and the blue haze that clouded the image of the distant future billowed from the fireman, but not the angel. "I'm sorry," both Barnabas and the fireman said, for two different reasons.

Behind the fireman, I could see an ambulance. The lights were off and I felt my life end when they put a small, covered body into it. The sheet was pulled over it all the way. For an instant, she didn't know what that meant, but I'd been in a body bag before, and somehow, when nothing I was thinking could reach her, this did.

"Oh, Johnny!" we sobbed as the reality hit her. In my vision, I started to cry as I watched the flames eat the roof of my room, but my tears were for Johnny. He was gone, and I cried for both Johnny and his sister as I had a vision of his round face and Transformer pajamas. He'd had fish sticks for dinner. I had been so mean, eating the last one when I knew he wanted it.

"I'm so sorry. I'm so sorry," I sobbed, my throat tight as I hunched against the bleacher support/side of the fire truck. Nearby was a fireman, giving me half his attention so I wouldn't run away. Nakita was superimposed on him, making sure no one came close enough to know what was going on. Behind her, the blue sun shone down on the track meet. They were preparing to set up the next race amid the blaring of loudspeakers and the honking of trucks as a new water tanker came in. My brother was dead. It was my fault. I shouldn't have left him alone.

I got up, or at least I did in my vision. I was starting to find the way to dissociate myself from it so I could just watch, making the heartache in the girl easier to bear. Barnabas holding me might have had something to do with it, too.

My fingers traced the name of the city on the fire truck: BAXTER, CA. My gaze rose and I saw the street sign: CORAL WAY. My heart pounded as I realized I had some control of this memory that had yet to be lived.

"Here you go, Tammy," a smoke-smudged man said, draping a blanket smelling of too much fabric softener over my shoulders. I shivered, unable to speak, but I had a name now, and that would help. "Your mom is coming," he added, and Tammy's panic slid through me anew.

Oh, God. Mom. I turned to the fire in a panic. I wanted to undo this, but I couldn't. Johnny was dead. It should be me there, not him. Not him!

"Madison?" Nakita said, and I blinked at the man as his features melted into hers. "Are you all right?"

I had to run away, leave. Facing this was too awful, and the guilt made it hard to breathe. *I should be dead, not Johnny. He was my brother, and now he is dead. Because of me. It should have been me. It should have been me!*

"Madison!"

Barnabas was calling my name, and I gasped as the two realities—one real, one yet to be lived—clashed violently. The blue tint flashed red, and then the future vanished.

The echo of my heart pounded, and I stilled it as I stared up at Barnabas, Nakita, and . . . Josh. Above me, people cheered the last runner to cross the line. It was over. I had flashed into someone else, lived the foretold death-strike of her soul, and . . . survived.

I swayed, trying to shake the guilt and heartache over the girl's brother's death. Tammy. Her name was Tammy. Her belief that she caused her brother's death still rang in me, a despair so heavy that it crushed all else and denied her soul the love it needed to survive. She would run, mentally if not physically, from those who would help her live again, and her soul . . . would wither and die long before her body did. Fate, the seraphs called it, but I didn't believe in fate.

The old dark timekeeper, Kairos, would have sent Nakita to kill Tammy without a thought, taking her soul to save it at the expense of her life. Ron, the current light timekeeper, would, in turn, send a light reaper to stop the scything, saving her life at the cost of her soul, gambling that she would somehow learn to live again. But I wasn't the old dark timekeeper, and I was going to use the opportunity to prove to the seraphs that fate could be sidestepped and we could save her life as well as her soul. All we needed to do was show Tammy a different choice.